# Katie
## just
## desserts

SIMON SPOTLIGHT

An imprint of Simon & Schuster Children's Publishing Division

1230 Avenue of the Americas, New York, New York 10020

First Simon Spotlight paperback edition September 2016

Copyright © 2016 by Simon & Schuster, Inc.

All rights reserved, including the right of reproduction

in whole or in part in any form.

SIMON SPOTLIGHT and colophon are registered trademarks of

Simon & Schuster, Inc.

Text by Tracey West

Chapter header illustrations and design by Laura Roode

For information about special discounts for bulk purchases, please contact

Simon & Schuster Special Sales at 1-866-506-1949

or business@simonandschuster.com.

Manufactured in the United States of America 0816 OFF

2 4 6 8 10 9 7 5 3 1

ISBN 978-1-4814-6878-7 (pbk)

ISBN 978-1-4814-6879-4 (hc)

ISBN 978-1-4814-6880-0 (eBook)

Library of Congress Control Number 2016947130

CUPCAKE DIARIES

# Katie
## just
## desserts

by coco simon

Simon Spotlight

New York    London    Toronto    Sydney    New Delhi

# CHAPTER 1

## S'More Surprises

Steady, Mia," I told one of my best friends.

That's because Mia Vélaz-Cruz was using a blowtorch, which is unusual for Mia since she's more likely to be holding a makeup brush or a sketch pencil or a sewing needle. She's very creative and artistic. And that's what she was using the blowtorch for—to make art. Out of cake frosting.

The community college near our town, Maple Grove, had announced a baking contest a few weeks ago for kids ages ten to seventeen. You had to first send in a recipe for a cake, and if your recipe was chosen, you were invited to the college to bake your cake in their kitchens in the final contest round.

As soon as Mia and I heard about the contest,

we knew we wanted to enter. We're part of a cupcake baking business with our friends Alexis Becker and Emma Taylor called the Cupcake Club. Emma knew she had a modeling gig the day of the contest, and Alexis had a school business club fair she was helping to run, so Mia and I entered together.

Each baker was allowed one helper, and Mia and I agreed that I should bake and she should help. We're a good team that way. I am food obsessed, so I'm good at coming up with recipes. And Mia can make any food look mouthwateringly delicious.

So, the recipe I came up with was a s'mores cake—a chocolate cake with layers of fudge and crumbled graham crackers in between. But the best part of the cake was the marshmallow frosting, which would top the cake with soft, fluffy peaks and then be browned with a blowtorch for that toasted marshmallow taste.

When Mia and I submitted the recipe, we hadn't thought too much about the blowtorch part. It looked easy when chefs used them on TV. But in real life, a blowtorch is kind of scary.

Luckily, monitors from the college were walking around the kitchens, making sure none of us kids were hurting ourselves with knives or stoves—or blowtorches. One of them rushed over quickly when he saw Mia holding the blowtorch.

"Do you know how to use that?" he asked.

"My stepdad, Eddie, showed me how," Mia replied. "He said it's the wimpiest blowtorch he could find, and I just have to twist it a tiny bit to let the flame come out. Like this."

Mia twisted the end, and a small flame burst from the torch.

The monitor nodded. "Good job," he said.

As he looked on, Mia carefully burned the tips of the marshmallow peaks so they turned a toasty brown color. Soon, our kitchen smelled just like a campfire!

"That's perfect, Mia!" I cried, clapping, and I saw the monitor smile.

An announcement came over the loudspeaker. "Five minutes until judging!"

I looked around our kitchen area. The college had a teaching kitchen for their cooking students. We each had a stainless-steel table as a work area, and an oven. Right now, our table was strewn with flour, powdered chocolate, and some spilled egg whites.

"I'll clean this up," I said. "Mia, just make the cake look as beautiful as possible!"

"You got it," Mia replied. "Katie, it already looks

and smells awesome. I think we could win."

As I straightened up, I glanced at the competition. Nine other contestants had made it to the finals. A few of the kids looked younger than Mia and I, who are in middle school. Most of the kids looked like they were in high school. And I had to admit, some of the cakes looked amazing. This one girl had a white layer cake with these beautiful flowers and butterflies made out of fondant, a paste made out of sugar, all over it.

"I don't know," I said. "Some of the cakes out there look incredible."

"Well, I think it all comes down to a matter of personal taste with these things, sometimes," Mia said. "Who are the judges, again?"

"There are five judges," I told her. "Two are professors here at the college, and then they got three food experts from the community. That's what the entry form said. I didn't read it too carefully."

I'm not exactly what you'd call a detail-oriented person. I knew that I had to make an amazing cake and that the prize was five hundred dollars. That's all I needed to know, right?

I noticed that I was nervously tapping my purple sneaker on the floor. I took a deep breath. This was it! We had baked our hearts out. I knew my cake was delicious. And thanks to Mia, it was beautiful. There was nothing left to do but wait to be judged.

I glanced at my station. The stainless steel gleamed brightly, and the cake looked perfect on a black pedestal cake stand. There wasn't a stray crumb or fleck of icing anywhere.

Mia looked around. "Do you think this is what it will be like when you go to cooking school?"

"I guess," I said. (Mia and I have a dream: After high school, we would both go to school in Manhattan. I would train to be a chef at one of the big cooking schools in New York, and Mia would go to one of the fashion schools there.) "This is a pretty nice kitchen. I don't know if the school in New York will be fancier than this."

"This is good practice, anyway," Mia said. "We should enter the contest every year."

Then we heard another announcement. "Let the judging begin!"

A bunch of judges wearing white chef's coats entered the kitchen. A woman with a blond ponytail approached our table first. She was smiling and looked nice, so I relaxed a little—just a little.

"'S'mores Cake,'" she said, reading aloud from the recipe card posted at our station. "What a clever idea. I was a Girl Scout, you know."

Mia nudged me, and we were both thinking the same thing. We had definitely won this judge over!

She carefully cut a thin slice of cake, put it on a plate, and took a bite.

"Very moist," she said. "The cookie crumble adds some nice texture. And the toasted marshmallow is wonderful."

"Thank you!" Mia and I said together, and I felt like I was beaming from head to toe.

The next judge was a short woman who wore her brown hair in a bun. She didn't smile at us. She read the recipe card and then tasted the cake. She nodded, put down the plate, and then started writing in a little pad. She didn't say a word to us!

"Oh boy," Mia said as the second judge walked away. "Does that mean she didn't like it?"

"I'm not sure," I whispered back. "Maybe that's just her judging style."

The next judge who walked up was a tall guy with dark hair. He looked vaguely familiar. And then I noticed his name tag: MARC DONALD BROWN.

That's when the whole world froze around me.

Marc Donald Brown is my dad.

My dad, who left my mom and me when I was really little.

My dad, who moved back to New Jersey recently with a whole new family.

My dad, who e-mailed me saying he wanted to meet me, but I turned him down. I wasn't ready.

And here he was, judging my cake.

Marc Donald Brown was smiling when he came to the table. Then he looked at me. I was wearing a name tag too: KATIE BROWN.

Marc Donald Brown got a weird look on his face. We both stared at each other.

Then my legs took on a life of their own. Some primal instinct took over and I ran. I ran as fast as I could out of that room, and I didn't look back.

# CHAPTER 2

## So Awkward!

*I* stood outside in the college courtyard, gasping for air. I fumbled for my cell phone in my apron pocket and dialed the number of my mom's dental practice.

"Oh, hey, Katie," Joanne, the receptionist, said cheerfully.

"Can I talk to her?" I asked.

"Sorry, your mom's in the middle of a tooth extraction," Joanne said. "Are you okay? You sound upset."

"No, no, I'm . . ." I couldn't quite bring myself to say I was fine. Because I definitely wasn't.

"I'll have her call you back as soon as she gets out, okay, hon?" Joanne asked.

"Yeah, sure," I said. I ended the call and sat

down on a bench. I needed a moment to think.

Mia raced up to me.

"Oh my gosh, Katie! I wasn't sure why you ran out, but then I saw the name on the judge, and I figured it out," she said. She put her arm around me. "You must be freaking out."

"I am," I said. I looked at her. "Mia, I'm sorry. I can't go back in there. Forget the contest. Let's just go home, okay?" My eyes started to fill with tears as I talked.

Mia nodded. "Of course. I'll call my mom to pick us up. I left my cell phone inside. I'll be right back."

Mia ran inside, and I took some deep breaths, trying to process.

When Marc Donald Brown had first e-mailed me, he said he wanted us to meet and talk. He wanted me to meet his family. I just couldn't do it. For one thing, I wasn't sure how I felt about a dad who took off and then waited more than an entire decade before trying to see me again. Yeah, he sent birthday cards and stuff, but that's about it.

And what did he do in that time? The guy who apparently couldn't handle having a wife and a baby went out and found a *new* wife and then had three more babies—all girls. I know because Mia and I

9

had this crazy idea to visit my dad's restaurant in Stonebrook, Chez Donald. (It's named that because he's always gone by his middle name, Donald.) I guess I thought I could maybe spy on my dad or something first, to see what he was like.

But I didn't even stay that long. I saw a newspaper article on the wall. I still remember the title. FAMILY MAN BRINGS FRENCH CUISINE TO STONEBROOK. There was a photo of Marc Donald Brown with his new wife and three little girls. No mention of me at all, but why would there be? I freaked out and ran out of the restaurant—just like I had done in the college kitchen.

"Katie?"

A man's voice interrupted my thoughts. Marc Donald Brown was standing there.

"Uh, hi," I said. My heart was pounding like crazy.

"Mind if I sit down?" he asked.

"No, sure," I said. I couldn't look him in the face. I just couldn't. I looked down at my apron and kept fumbling with the strings.

"I'm sure this must be awkward for you," he said. "It's awkward for me."

*Majorly awkward!* I thought, but I didn't say anything.

"I didn't know you were going to be in this contest," he said. "Otherwise, I would have tried to reach out beforehand."

"I didn't know you were going to be a judge," I mumbled.

"I still want to get to know you, Katie," MDB said. "Not like this, though."

"Oh, but you're such a family man," I found myself saying, remembering the article. "Don't you need to spend time with your other three daughters?"

"This is the kind of stuff we need to talk about," he said. "Just please consider it. We can meet somewhere, just the two of us. There's a lot I need to say to you."

Something in his voice made me look up. His green eyes looked kind of sad.

"I'll think about it," I said.

"Okay," MDB said. He stood up. "By the way, your cake was delicious."

*Does he really think that, or is he just saying that?* I wondered. Something inside me really hoped he was being sincere. For some weird reason, it was important that Marc Donald Brown knew I was a good baker. That I was good at something.

Mia walked toward me as he walked away, and

she raised her eyebrows. "You okay?" she asked.

"I guess," I said. "He still wants to meet with me. I'm not sure if I want to, though. It's so weird!"

"Yeah, I can't imagine," Mia said.

I knew she couldn't. Mia's parents were divorced, like mine, but her dad never left the picture. Mia goes and stays with him in Manhattan every other weekend, and she spends half the summer with him, too. He's not some stranger, like Marc Donald Brown.

Mia and I didn't talk anymore. We were quiet until her mom came to pick us up. Mrs. Valdes smiled and said hi, but then she didn't say anything either, so I knew Mia had told her what happened.

"Katie, you know you're welcome to come to our house for dinner," Mia's mom said as we got closer to my house.

"Thanks, I'm okay," I said. When the car pulled up, I muttered a good-bye and quickly ran out, let myself into my house, and then headed straight up to my bedroom.

Then I threw myself on my bed and cried and cried, and I wasn't even really sure why.

# CHAPTER 3

## Decisions, Decisions

I didn't even hear Mom's key turn in the lock, and I didn't hear her walk upstairs, either. The first thing I noticed was her hand on my back.

"Katie, what's wrong?" she asked. "Did you lose the contest?"

*The contest.* I had forgotten all about that, actually. I sat up and wiped away my tears.

For a second I stared at Mom's face. I always thought that she and I looked alike. We both had brown hair, even though mine was long and messy and hers was short and bouncy, and brown eyes. But now I wondered. Marc Donald Brown had brown hair. Did I look like him, too?

"It's not the contest," I said finally. "I left the contest."

"You left? Why?" Mom asked.

"Because Marc Donald Brown was one of the judges," I told her.

Mom's eyes got wide. "Oh," she said. Then she hugged me. "Oh, Katie. That must have been so upsetting for you. I'm sorry."

I felt the tears coming again, but I held them back.

"I ran out," I told her. "He came out to talk to me. He asked me to meet with him again. But I'm not sure if I want to."

Mom sighed. "So you ran out, and he came out to find you?" she asked.

I nodded.

"Well, that was decent of him," Mom said. "I do worry about you getting hurt, hon, and I'm sure you do too."

"Yeah," I said. "I mean, why does he want to see me after all this time? Isn't he busy enough with his other three daughters?"

*And what if he doesn't like me as much as he likes them?* I added to myself. What if he meets me and then never wants to see me again?

"I know it must hurt that he has another family," Mom said. "But I think it's a good thing that he wants to reconnect with you, Katie. It's up to you, but maybe it will be good for you. It might give you a chance to work out this chapter of your life."

Mom was making sense. I thought about all those years that I had wondered what it would be like to have a dad who did things with me. Wondered why my dad had left. Maybe if I talked to him, I'd get some answers.

"I might do it," I told her. "I'm just not sure yet."

"Let me know," Mom said. "And if you want me to reach out to him, I will."

I hugged her. "Thanks, Mom."

Mom kissed me on the forehead. "I think we could both use some Chinese takeout."

"Vegetable lo mein," I said. "And chicken with broccoli. And wonton soup. And an egg roll."

Mom laughed. "That's my Katie. Don't worry. I'll get us a feast. And then maybe we can go for a run in the morning."

Mom left to call in our order, and I went to the bathroom to splash water on my face. I felt a lot better. This whole thing with Marc Donald Brown was pretty stressful. But I could always count on Mom to make things right.

I was feeling even better the next day, especially after spending a fun night with Mom, eating

Chinese food and watching a movie in our pj's, and then going for a run the next morning. You would think that when you're running, you'd have nothing to do but think about your problems rolling around in your head, but for me, it's just the opposite. When I'm running, all my problems fly out of my head. My mind focuses on the *thump-thump* of my feet against the path in the park and the birds flitting and swooping from tree to tree.

I did some homework for the rest of the day and then chilled out before my Cupcake Club meeting that night. Mom made us chicken soup and grilled cheese sandwiches for dinner, and then she dropped me off at Mia's house.

There was an amazing smell coming from her house, and when Mia opened the door for me, the smell got stronger. I waited for her little white dogs, Tiki and Milkshake, to stop yapping and jumping on me before I asked her about it.

"Eddie made this amazing chicken for dinner," Mia explained. "Chicken breasts rolled up with stuff inside and then cooked in delicious sauce."

Eddie came out of the kitchen just then. "It's called a roulade," he explained. "I saw it on a cooking show. But you probably know all about roulades, Katie, since you're such a good cook yourself."

I felt myself blushing a little. "Yeah, we made them at cooking camp during the summer."

"Then you have to try mine!" he said, grabbing me by the arm. "I need your expert opinion."

*Sorry,* Mia mouthed as he pulled me into the kitchen, but I didn't mind. Eddie is Mia's stepdad, and he's supernice. He's always ready to help the Cupcake Club, whether we need a ride somewhere or extra hands to help frosting cupcakes.

Eddie took one of the roulades off a platter on the counter and put it on plate, then placed it on the table along with a knife and fork.

"Sit, eat!" he said. "Your meeting hasn't started yet."

"Yes, but it's going to start soon, so don't keep Katie forever," Mia told him. "I've got to set up for the meeting."

"This smells great, so it won't last long," I promised.

Even though I had eaten dinner already, the smell of the dish made me hungry, and I dug in. Mia was right. It was yummy, stuffed with spinach and cheese and topped with a creamy sauce.

"This is soooo good," I told Eddie after a few bites. "The chicken comes out supermoist when you cook it this way. There's nothing worse than dry chicken."

Eddie beamed. "Excellent! Now I've got the Katie Seal of Approval! Now, please excuse me while I start the dishes."

As I finished the chicken, I couldn't help thinking how lucky Mia was to have such a nice step-dad. And she was double lucky, because her real dad was just as nice too. So Mia had *two* dads, and all I had was a Marc Donald Brown. So, when the universe was giving out dads, why did I get short-changed? It was kind of not fair.

I heard the doorbell ring and the dogs yap, and I knew that Alexis and Emma had arrived. I got up and handed Eddie my plate.

"Thanks so much," I said. "That was awesome."

"You're very welcome. I'm glad you liked it!" Eddie said.

I joined Mia in the dining room, which was set up for our meeting with a pitcher of water, some glasses, and a plate of homemade cookies that I guessed Eddie had probably made for us.

"Yay, cookies!" Emma cheered, taking a seat.

Alex sat next to her, placing a stuffed (but neat) binder down on the table in front of her.

"Wow, Alexis, your hair looks cute," Mia remarked. Alexis had pulled her wavy red hair into a thick side braid. It was a new look for Alexis.

"Thanks," Alexis said. "Sometimes it's nice not to have to keep brushing my hair away from my face, you know?"

"I know," agreed Mia, who often wore her glossy dark hair slicked back in a neat ponytail. (I like to wear my hair in a ponytail too, especially when I'm baking. But it never looks as neat as Mia's.)

Alexis opened her binder. "So, exciting news," she said. "Did you guys see that new magazine office that opened up downtown?"

"*New Jersey* something, right?" Emma asked.

"It's called *Relish New Jersey*, and it's a food and lifestyle magazine," Alexis explained. "They're launching their first issue in a few weeks, and they want to hire us to make the cupcakes!"

"Wow, so how did they find out about us?" I asked.

Alexis grinned. "It might have something to do with that letter and flyer I sent them," she said.

We high-fived. "Way to get the business, Alexis!" I said.

Then she put on her serious face. "So, the editor wants a cupcake that speaks to the latest food trends," she said. "I did some research, and it's clear that the top new trend is vegetables in desserts."

Emma made a face. "Ew!"

Alexis passed out a sheet of paper with examples to each of us.

"'Sweet potato ice cream,'" I read out loud. "'Candied kale chips.'"

"Double ew!" said Emma.

"I don't know," I said. "It sounds kind of interesting."

Mia was frowning. "How can you make vegetable cupcakes look pretty?" she asked.

"Well, I think we can make it work," Alexis said. "Let's all think about it before our next meeting. And, Emma, if you can come up with a different trend, we'll consider it."

"Oh, I'll be looking for one," Emma promised.

"All right, now let's talk about our budget," Alexis said.

Budget stuff is definitely not the most exciting thing about running a cupcake business, but it's important, and I'm glad Alexis is good at it. When we finished that, and started talking about other stuff besides cupcakes, I decided I should tell Alexis and Emma about what happened with Marc Donald Brown.

"So I totally freaked out and left the contest," I explained. "I'm so glad I had Mia there with me."

"I'm glad I was there too," said Mia.

"Oh, Katie, that's just awful," said Emma. "What a weird coincidence!"

"I don't know," Alexis said. "Your dad owns a popular restaurant close by. I guess there was always a chance that you would run into each other sometime."

I nodded. "Yeah, in a way it was easier when he was living across the country and I didn't have to think about him so much."

"And now you have to think about him all the time," said Emma.

"So what are you going to do?" Alexis asked. "Are you going to meet him?"

"I'm still not sure," I said.

"Well, I think you should do it," Alexis said. "If you don't like him, you never have to meet him again. But at least you'll stop wondering."

"That makes sense," agreed Mia. "I know it will be hard, but at least you'll get it over with, and you won't have to keep worrying about it."

"I think it's okay as long as you don't feel uncomfortable doing it," added Emma.

So there it was. My three best friends thought I should meet with my dad. So did my mom.

"Okay," I said. "I'll do it."

When I got home from the meeting, I talked to Mom first thing.

"So, I think I want to meet with Marc Donald Brown," I said. "Can I send him an e-mail?"

Mom raised an eyebrow a little bit, but that might have been because I was calling my dad by his full name. I usually referred to him as "Dad," but somehow that didn't feel right anymore, not since he e-mailed about meeting up with me. Why should I call him Dad when he'd never been a father to me? Now, in my head, he was Marc Donald Brown.

"You feel okay doing this?" she asked, and I nodded.

"Then get your laptop," Mom replied.

With Mom looking over my shoulder, I typed in the message.

Hi, it's Katie. Maybe we can meet on Saturday somewhere. E-mail me back.

"Is that all what you want to say?" she asked.

I stared at the e-mail. Actually, there was lots of stuff I wanted to add.

*Maybe you can explain why you haven't been in my life.*

*This is totally weird for me.*

*If you don't like me, just pretend that you do so it won't hurt my feelings.*

"No, this is good," I said.

I pressed send, and that was that.

The next move was up to Marc Donald Brown.

# CHAPTER 4

## Achoo!

When I woke up the next morning, my throat felt like it was on fire. It hurt to swallow. And my nose was all stuffed up. I tried to breathe, but I had to do it through my mouth. And that just made my throat hurt more.

I groaned and pulled a pillow over my head. I had a cold! *How did I get a cold overnight?* I wondered. Well, there was no way I was going to school. I closed my eyes and fell back asleep. I knew my mom would come looking for me when I didn't come down to breakfast, and I'd tell her then I was sick. I didn't have the energy to get up and tell her myself.

When I opened my eyes again, my digital clock read 9:10. I bolted awake. Why hadn't Mom come in to see me yet? School had already started!

"Mom?" I called out in a scratchy voice.

There was no answer.

Worried, I got up and walked to her room. The door was half-open, and when I peeked inside, I saw Mom in bed, snoring loudly.

"Mom?"

Mom's eyes opened. She shot up in bed.

"Oh gosh, Katie, I'm sorry!" she said. Her voice sounded scratchy, and her nose sounded stuffy, just like mine. "I have a cold and I feel awful. I started to get up to make you breakfast, and then I thought I'd tell you to make yourself cereal, and I just fell asleep."

"It's okay," I said, climbing into bed next to her. "I'm sick too."

"Poor Katie!" Mom said, hugging me. "I'll get up and call the school and tell them you're not going. Then I'll make us both some tea and toast and get out the vitamins and the cold medicine."

"Thanks, Mom," I said, snuggling under her covers.

I hadn't climbed into bed with Mom since I was little and was scared by a bad thunderstorm. My new puppy, Snickerdoodle, jumped on the bed and cuddled up next to me. It felt nice.

I started to doze off again, and Mom came back with some hot tea and toast, like she'd promised. We ate in bed, and then I closed my eyes and fell asleep some more.

When I opened them again, Mom was up and dressed in sweatpants and a T-shirt.

"I think it's time we moved Cold Central downstairs," she said. She felt my forehead to see if I had a fever. "Let's watch some TV. And you can bring down your laptop and check to see if you're missing any homework today."

"Can we have soup?" I asked.

Mom frowned. "I checked. We're all out. We'll have to settle for P-B-and-Js. But I'll make some more tea."

A little while later we were set up in the living room under blankets that my grandma Carole had crocheted for us. Mom's was blue and green, and mine was every color of the rainbow because Grandma knows I like crazy colors.

After we ate our P-B-and-Js I got out my laptop, like Mom had suggested. Before I checked the school's website, I checked my e-mail. There, in my in-box, was a reply from Marc Donald Brown.

*"Achoo!"* I sneezed right when I saw the e-mail. Then I clicked on it.

Katie, I am so glad that you are willing to meet. Can we meet at Lane's on Main at 11:00 on Saturday morning? Let me know if this works for you. I'm happy to change the time or place if it doesn't.

Lane's on Main is a coffee shop here in Maple Grove. Before I typed back a message, I turned to Mom.

"Marc Donald Brown says he can meet at Lane's on Main at eleven on Saturday," I told her.

"Okay," Mom said. "I'm not working, so I can take you."

"*Achoo!* Thanks, Mom," I said. I guess I should have started to feel nervous about meeting Marc Donald Brown, but I wasn't—not yet. I was probably just too busy being sick.

I e-mailed him back that it was okay, and then Mom and I settled in to watch TV. Luckily, Mom likes watching cartoon channels just as much as I do, and there's nothing like being sick and watching silly cartoons. So even though I felt terrible I was pretty content.

Mia texted me around 3:00, after school was out. Katie! U okay? Where are u?

Bad cold, I typed back, and then I sent an emoji

27

of a sneezing smiley face. Hope you don't get it.

I'll be okay, Mia said. Miss u!

Then Mia and I started texting back and forth about what had happened that day in school. I was still texting when the doorbell rang.

"Who could that be?" I asked.

"I don't know," Mom said. She walked to the door and peeked through the small window at the top. Then she smiled. "It's Jeff!"

So, Jeff Green is my mom's boyfriend. He's also a math teacher at my school. At home, I call him Jeff. At school, I call him Mr. Green.

"Hey, there," Jeff said as he walked in. He had a shopping bag in each hand. "How are things in the sick ward?"

"Sore and stuffy," Mom supplied. "You really should get out of here. I don't want you to get sick!"

"I'm a teacher. Our bodies build up cold and flu defenses after being around runny noses and sniffles day after day," he said. "Anyway, I brought you some soup."

"Soup!" I cried happily. "*Achoo!* Thanks!"

"You're welcome," Jeff said. "I got it from Kleiner's deli. Chicken and matzo ball. It's the best. Now, sit back and let me take care of you two."

He walked into the kitchen, and I could hear him moving things around. Mom shrugged and got back onto the couch with me.

A few minutes later Jeff came in with two bowls of soup on a tray and set them down in front of us.

"Be right back," he said as we picked up the yummy-smelling, steaming soup.

He returned a moment later. "Okay, so I got the tissues with the lotion in them," he said, putting some boxes down on the coffee table. "And I can see they're just in time. Your noses are so red!"

"The lotion tissues are awesome," I said. "Thanks."

Then he handed me the latest issue of *Cooking Monthly*, and Mom got a home decorating magazine.

"My dad always used to bring me a comic book when I was sick," he said. "I wasn't sure if you liked comic books, though."

I eagerly picked up the cooking magazine. It's got tons of great recipes and cool pictures. I'd been wanting to subscribe to it, but lately I've been spending my Cupcake money on baking supplies.

"This is better than a comic book," I told him.

Jeff smiled. He straightened out Mom's blanket and then pulled it over her legs and tucked in the edges underneath. He did the same for me.

"Anything else I can do for you guys?" he asked.

"No, thank you, honey," Mom said. "This was so sweet of you. I'm so happy you stopped by. Love you."

"Love you, too," Jeff said. "Call me if you need anything. I'll let myself out."

Jeff left, and I turned to Mom.

"'Love you'?" I repeated.

Mom blushed. "Yes, we have grown to love each other," she said. "It's nice."

I let that sink in. Mom and Jeff loved each other. A few months ago I might have been worried about that—worried that Mom might not have enough love for both me and Jeff. But now I was pretty sure that she did.

"Cool," I said. Then I put down my soup and snuggled under my blanket. This was so nice of him.

"It was," Mom agreed.

I thought about what Jeff had said—about how his dad had always brought him a comic book when he got sick. And now he was doing the same thing for us. Not just for Mom, but for me, too. Just like a father would do.

I closed my eyes and tried to imagine Marc

Donald Brown bringing me soup or tucking a blanket around my legs.

I couldn't. Then I started to wonder if he did those things for his three perfect little blond daughters. . . . I didn't want to think about it.

"Katie, look! It's *Captain Cookie's Happy Hour*!" Mom said, turning up the volume on the TV with glee.

That was great timing. Because instead of going into a dark place, I got swept up into the wacky cartoon world of Captain Cookie. Trust me—that was a much better place to be!

# CHAPTER 5

# A Special Assignment?

By Wednesday morning I was back at school and feeling better. Well, almost better.

"Okay, so determine the ratio of twenty-four to sixty for me," Mr. K., my math teacher, was saying. "Remember, you need to find the greatest common factor for each number."

I stared down at my paper. I had been sick of hanging out on the couch and was all fired up to get back to school, and then—*bam!* First-period math. Suddenly, the couch didn't seem so bad.

Now, I have gotten a lot better at math since I started middle school. Alexis is always willing to help me, and I've got a secret study weapon in Jeff. But tackling ratios right after coming back from a cold. Um, no.

But I got through it, and my next class is Spanish, which I really like. I'd love to go to Mexico someday and learn cooking from some of the chefs there, and knowing Spanish would be really helpful. When I get to high school, I want to take French, too, because all the best chefs train in Paris. At least that's what I've read.

Next came gym class, and I lucked out because Ms. Chen was doing two weeks of yoga lessons with us. So instead of running around and getting all sweaty, I got to breathe and stretch. Nice.

After gym I walked with Mia, Emma, and Alexis to the cafeteria.

"We missed you, Katie," Alexis said. "Were you able to research any cupcake flavors while you were out?"

I shook my head. "Sorry, I was a total lump for the last two days," I said. "I mostly watched cartoons. But I'll get on it."

Then I remembered something.

"Oh yeah, and I got an e-mail from Marc Donald Brown," I told my friends. "I'm going to meet him on Saturday."

"Get out!" Emma stopped in the hallway and turned to face me. "That's great. But you must be so nervous."

I nodded. "Yeah, a little bit."

"I'll be with my dad on Saturday, but you can text me if you need me," Mia offered.

"Yeah, and Emma and I will be around if you need us," Alexis added.

"Thanks, guys," I said.

When we got to the cafeteria, Alexis and Emma got in line to get their lunch, and Mia and I claimed our usual table. I unpacked my lunch. Mom had given me a thermos of tomato soup (I was still on a soup kick) with some whole wheat crackers and cheese. Yum!

Alexis and Emma joined us a few minutes later, carrying their trays. Both of them had big salads with veggies and chicken.

"Wow, the school lunches are looking better lately," Mia remarked.

Emma nodded. "Yeah, there's a lot more green stuff to choose from," she said. "And I like green stuff. Just not in my cupcakes."

She looked pointedly at Alexis.

"Listen, I'm not saying we have to make broccoli cupcakes or anything," Alexis said. "But we've got to pay attention to trends, and this is one of them."

"So when are we meeting next?" I asked.

"Can we do Sunday night?" Mia asked. "We can do it at my house again."

Alexis scrolled through her phone to check her schedule. "That works, as long as you don't mind."

"No, it's easier," said Mia. "I'll be getting back from Manhattan around three, and I can chill out a little before the meeting starts."

"I hope you're talking about a Cupcake meeting."

Mr. Green had approached us. Teachers take turns monitoring the cafeteria, and I guess today was his turn.

"As a matter of fact, we are," Alexis replied. "Are there any cupcake needs we can help you with?"

"As a matter of fact, there is," Mr. Green replied. "I have a special assignment for the Cupcake Club, but I can't talk about it here. Would it be okay if I came to your next meeting?"

Mia, Alexis, Emma, and I all looked at one another. Mr. Green was acting very mysteriously.

"I don't see why not," replied Alexis. She started typing into her phone. "Our next Cupcake Club meeting starts at seven this Sunday, so why don't you come at seven fifteen?"

Mr. Green grinned. "Sounds great. Where should I go?"

"It's at my house," Mia said, and Mr. Green nodded. He had been to Mia's house before, to have dinner with Mom and me and Mia's family.

"I'll see you then," he said. Then he looked at me. "You look much better, Katie. I'm glad to see that."

"I still can't believe you didn't get sick," I told him.

"I told you, superteacher antibodies," he said. "Plus, I take my vitamins." Then he walked off, whistling.

"What was *that* about?" Emma wondered aloud.

"Honestly, I have no idea," I said.

"He seems very happy," Mia remarked.

"You're right," agreed Alexis. "Katie, have you noticed that?"

"He's always been a pretty chill guy," I said, which was true, and then suddenly, I remembered what my mom had told me. That she and Jeff loved each other. Could that have something to do with it? Maybe, but I didn't exactly feel like sharing that information in the middle of the cafeteria.

"Well, I guess we'll find out Sunday," Emma said, picking at her lettuce with a fork.

"We'll find out a lot on Sunday," Alexis added. "We'll finally know what your father's like, Katie."

"Yeah, I guess we will," I said, and then I started slurping my soup so I wouldn't have to talk about it anymore.

My meeting with my dad was only a few days away. The nervousness started to bubble up inside me. The way I saw it, the meeting could only go two ways:

It could be amazing, with me and Marc Donald Brown instantly bonding and talking and laughing like we had been part of each other's lives forever. We would both love hot chocolate and we would finish each other's sentences and realize that we had so much in common.

Or it could be awful, with him making up some lame excuse about why he had left and me freaking out and running out of the coffee shop and him deciding it wasn't worth having a relationship with a crazy daughter like me.

I was convinced the meeting would be either totally amazing or a total disaster. It never occurred to me that it might be something in between.

# CHAPTER 6

## Marc Donald Brown

How are you feeling, Katie?" Mom asked as she drove me to the coffee shop on Saturday morning.

I know she wasn't asking me about the after-effects of my cold. She was just as worried as I was about me meeting Marc Donald Brown. For the last few days I had caught her staring at me several times, like she was expecting to see me break down or cry at any minute.

"I'm okay," I said. But my stomach was doing little flip-flops when I said it.

"Well, I'll be close by," Mom said. "I'm not going back home; I'm going to do some shopping in town. So text me as soon as you want me to come get you, and I'll be there in a flash, okay?"

"Okay," I said. Then I had a funny thought. "Are

you really going to be shopping, or are you going to be spying on us through the window?"

Mom smiled. "Actually, my plan was to disguise myself as a barista and spy on you from inside the coffee shop," she said.

I laughed. "I can just see you doing that!"

Mom pulled into a spot in the municipal parking lot.

"Is your phone charged?" she asked.

I patted my pocket. "Charged all night."

She took a deep breath. "Okay, let's do this."

We got out of the car and walked toward Lane's on Main. It was a beautiful morning. We turned on to Main Street, which is filled with cute little shops—a candy shop, a toy shop, a pet boutique, and lots of clothing shops. Between Tanya's Treasures (a jewelry shop) and Footprints (a shoe store) was Lane's on Main.

There were a few people sitting at the round metal tables outside. Marc Donald Brown was standing by the front door, looking up and down the street. He waved when he saw us.

"Good morning, Sharon. Hi, Katie," he said as we walked up.

"Hey, Don," Mom said. She turned to me. "Katie, I need to talk to your dad for a minute before I leave you two. Why don't you go inside and find a table?"

I nodded. "Okay," I said.

Lane's on Main was crowded, but I managed to find a small table for two. It had a view of the window, and I watched Mom talking with Marc Donald Brown.

*Those are my parents,* I thought. My mom and dad. Together. What would my life have been like if they had stayed together? I wondered. I tried to imagine Marc Donald Brown eating Chinese food on the couch with Mom and me or running through the park with us. But I couldn't. It was weird.

Then Mom waved to me through the window, and Marc Donald Brown walked inside.

"Can I get you something, Katie?" he asked me. "Coffee? A cookie? They have great scones here."

"I'll take a hot chocolate, please," I said. "Thanks."

I stared out the window and nervously tapped my foot against the floor as he got our beverages. He came back with a mug of steaming hot chocolate for me and a cup of espresso for himself.

"So," he said, "thanks for meeting me."

I just nodded. I didn't know what to say. I waited for him to speak again. He was the one who was so eager to see me. I was going to let him do the talking.

He cleared his throat. "I just . . . I owe you an apology, Katie," he said. "Your mom and I were really young when we got together, and I was in a strange place in my life. My parents pushed me into dental school, but I didn't really want to go. I didn't know what I wanted to do. And then I met your mom."

He looked away, and I could tell he was thinking about a far-off memory.

"I really loved her—I did," he said. "But we got married, and then we had you, and it all happened so fast." He shook his head and took a sip of his espresso.

"And then you left," I blurted out.

MDB nodded. "I did. And I'm sorry. I hated being a dentist. It was my parents' dream, not mine. I had always wanted to be a chef. I worked my way through college in the kitchen of a restaurant."

"You did?" I asked. I had never heard that about him.

"Yes, and then one day, after you were born, a friend of mine from the restaurant called me. He was going to Paris to intern with a restaurant there, and he said he could get me in too. I couldn't believe it.

41

It was always what I had dreamed of doing. So . . . I left." He looked away from me.

"But why couldn't you have stayed married to Mom?" I asked. "Couldn't she have been a dentist in Paris? Or you could have had a long-distance relationship. And then after your internship ended, you could have come back here to be with us."

"That makes sense now, the way you're saying it, Katie," MDB said. "You're much more mature than I was when I was twenty-four. Back then, I didn't feel like I had those options. It felt, well, all-or-nothing to me. Like I had a chance to live the life that I wanted, finally."

My stomach felt hot. I know Marc Donald Brown was being honest with me. But I didn't much like what he had to say.

"A life without Mom and me, you mean?" I asked.

"Katie, it wasn't like that," he said. "Your mom thought I was crazy to want to be a chef. She wanted us to open up a practice together. We fought a lot over my decision."

"Mom told me you moved to Washington State," I told him.

"I did, eventually," MDB said. "After the Paris internship, I went to Spain and then Germany. I

42

was getting an education that I knew I couldn't get anywhere else. And while I was there . . . Well, I wasn't thinking too much about what I had left behind.

"In a kitchen in Germany, I met Jasmine—she's my wife," he said. "We moved back to the States to be closer to her family in the Pacific Northwest, and that's how I ended up in Washington."

*Jasmine.* The woman who had replaced my mom. I let that sink in. My mom had a good old-fashioned name: Sharon. Sharon was a good name for a dentist or a teacher or a nurse or a mom. Jasmine sounded like, well, a princess or a woman who created a line of cosmetics.

"We opened a restaurant in Olympia," he went on. "And then we had our three girls."

"I know," I said. "I read the newspaper article."

"They're part of the reason I reached out to you, Katie," he said. "Watching the three of them grow up . . . I started to realize how much I was missing by not seeing you grow up. And I want my girls to get to know their sister."

I let that sink in too. One minute I was Katie Brown, only child, and then—*boom!* Katie Brown, older sister of three.

He took out his phone.

"Would you like to see their picture?" he asked.

"Um, sure," I said, because I was genuinely curious. It had been a while since I'd seen that newspaper photo.

He brought up a picture and held out the phone to me. "The oldest is Cecile; she's eight," he said. "And Ella is six, and the youngest, Riley, is four."

I looked at their faces, searching for some resemblance to me. But they had Marc Donald Brown's green eyes, and that blond hair had to have come from Jasmine, I guessed.

"They're cute," I said, because I felt like I needed to say something polite. And it wasn't a lie. They *were* cute—I just wasn't sure how I felt about having half sisters yet.

MDB took the phone from me. "I'm not asking you to understand, Katie, or even for your forgiveness," he said. "But I felt like I owed you an explanation. And I want you to know that I'm sorry to have missed so much of your life already."

I was glad he said that. Something inside me softened up a tiny bit. Because if he had been expecting me to say, *Oh, it's okay; I understand; don't worry about it*, that was not going to happen.

"So," he said, "I would really like to get to know

you better. For starters, maybe you can tell me about this Cupcake Club."

"Well, it kind of started on my first day of middle school," I told him. "My best friend, Callie, dumped me. And at lunchtime I ate with Mia, this new girl who's now my best friend, and Alexis and Emma, who were already best friends. And Mom had packed me a peanut-butter-and-jelly cupcake, like she always does on the first day of school, and we started talking about cupcakes."

Marc Donald Brown nodded. "So you bonded over food. I get that."

Then I went on to explain how we had formed a business, and told him about some of the jobs that we had, and he asked me a lot of questions about where we got our supplies and how we budgeted our expenses.

"It sounds like you've got a nice little business going," he said. "And you and each of your friends bring something to the team. I'm guessing you come up with a lot of the recipes?"

I nodded. "That's my favorite part."

I was waiting for him to say, "Well, you got that from me," but he didn't—and I was glad that he didn't. Because that wouldn't have been fair. Mom is the one who taught me how to cook and how to bake cupcakes. Even if maybe I did get some cooking gene from Marc Donald Brown, Mom is the one who really encouraged my talent and helped me with it.

"I really would like to get you know you better, Katie," he said. "And I had a thought about that, which I passed by your mom. How would you like an internship with a pastry chef at my restaurant? Well, not an 'internship,' really, and I can't pay you, but it'll be a chance for you to observe how a kitchen in a restaurant works, help out a little with the prep work and baking, things like that. It'll be good experience for when you go to culinary school."

I was pretty shocked. Of all the things I had imagined happening at this meeting, me being offered an internship was not one of them. I didn't know what to say, so I just stared at him with my mouth open for a few seconds.

"Take your time and think about it, Katie," he said. "Our pastry chef, Melissa Stackman, is really good at what she does, and really nice besides. I think you'd have a good time. We could work out what times and days are best for you to come in that won't conflict with school or your cupcake business."

"Wow," I said. "That, um, sounds like an amazing opportunity. I should probably think about it, though."

And I really did need to think about it. I had always heard that the environment in a kitchen is fast-paced and crazy. Did I really want to get to know Marc Donald Brown under those circumstances? But then again, how else would we ever get to know each other? Certainly not by meeting for coffee every week.

And besides, interning at a restaurant (especially a well-reviewed one like Chez Donald) was a fantastic experience for someone my age. It would look great on a cooking school application, too.

Even so, the offer kind of felt like a sort of . . . consolation prize. *You don't get to have me as a father, but you can work in my restaurant!*

"Just let me know when you have your answer, Katie," Marc Donald Brown said. "And let me know if you'd like to meet your sisters soon."

"Half sisters," I corrected. "And I'll need to think about that, too."

I happened to glance over at the window then, and I saw Mom looking in. She wasn't exactly spying, but it was good to see her. I waved at her.

"Well, I guess I should go," I said, standing up.

I awkwardly stuck out my hand, because I wasn't sure of the best way to say good-bye, and that's the first thing my body thought of. A hug didn't seem quite right, but a handshake was kind of weird. Who shakes hands with their father? But Marc Donald Brown shook my hand and smiled.

Then I bolted out of the coffee shop and let out a long, slow breath.

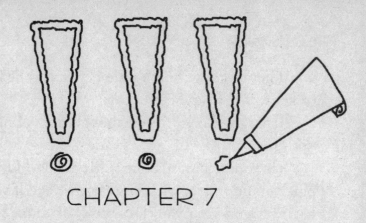

# CHAPTER 7

## It's Actually Happening!

"How did it go?" Mom asked after we climbed into the car.

"Okay, I guess," I said. "It was weird. And I guess you know he offered me an internship."

Mom nodded. "Yes. How do you feel about that?"

I had to think about it. "I'm kind of torn. It's a great opportunity. Like, if he weren't my dad, I would probably jump at it. But the fact that he is my dad . . . Well, that makes it kind of awkward. He hasn't been around all these years, and now he'll be my boss."

"I talked to him about that," Mom said. "He wouldn't be directly supervising you. You'll be working with the pastry chef, Melissa. So this way, you'd get to know him a little better, and he'll get to know you a little better too."

"It might work," I said thoughtfully. "I'm just not sure."

"It's your decision, honey," Mom said. "I'll support you no matter what you choose. And if you're having a hard time, you can always talk to me about it. Or talk to your friends. They always give you good advice."

I thought about how many problems Mia, Alexis, and Emma had helped me deal with. I don't know what I would have done without them!

"Good idea," I told Mom.

I thought about calling Mia right away, but I knew she was in Manhattan with her dad, and they usually do fun stuff together, like go to museums and fancy restaurants.

I was right. Mia texted me that night, late. How did things go with ur dad? Sorry I didn't text earlier. Dad took me to see *Wicked* on Broadway.

Sounds like fun! I texted back. Things went okay. I'll tell you more tomorrow.

Okay. Nite! ☺, Mia wrote.

I would have kept texting, but I had a lot to tell, and I didn't feel like typing everything out.

The next night, I waited till all my friends were

together at the Cupcake Club meeting to tell them all that had happened with my dad. We were back in Mia's house, sitting around the dining room table.

"So, we've got fifteen minutes until Mr. Green gets here with his mysterious request," Alexis said. "I thought we could go over our schedule for the next month before he gets here."

"Good idea, but first, I need to hear what happened when Katie met her dad yesterday," Mia said.

"Yes, that's right!" said Emma. "How did it go? Was it totally weird?"

I told them what had happened, ending with the part about him offering me an internship.

"You definitely should do it," Alexis said. "With that on your résumé, you'll get into any culinary school you want to."

Emma frowned. "I don't know. It sounds like it could be totally awkward."

"I think it's worth a try," Mia said. "It's a good opportunity, and if it gets weird, you could always just quit."

Believe it or not, I hadn't thought about that. "Thanks," I said. "I'm still not exactly sure what I want to do, but—"

Just then the doorbell rang, and Tiki and Milkshake started barking like crazy. A few seconds later Mia's mom came into the dining room with Jeff.

"Hey, girls," he said. "Thanks for letting me come to your meeting."

"I hope they give you a good deal," Mrs. Valdes said, winking at Jeff. I figured that whatever he was up to, she knew about it.

"Before we talk business, I'd like to have a word with Katie in the kitchen," he said.

"Uh, sure," I said, and I followed him out of the dining room as my friends looked on curiously.

Jeff turned to me and took a deep breath. "So, I was going to tell you this at the meeting, but then I realized that might not be the best thing to do. You deserve to hear this from me first."

I was starting to feel nervous. "Okay?"

He took another deep breath. "Katie, I'm going to ask your mom to marry me. And I want to propose to her with a cupcake. A special cupcake made by the Cupcake Club. But if that's weird for you, or you don't want to do it, I completely understand."

I couldn't breathe for a second. Jeff wanted to marry my mom! Of course, I knew that was probably going to happen. He and mom had talked about it. Mom had even explained to me that if she and Jeff got married, he would move into our house with us. And his daughter, Emily, would live with us sometimes.

And now it was happening! And the thought of Mom and Jeff getting married made me feel happy but also kind of scared, too. I still worried that things would never be the same again with Mom and me once she married Jeff.

And now Jeff wanted the Cupcake Club to help him propose. Which was sweet, really. And he had told me first!

I noticed Jeff was staring at me, and I realized that I hadn't said a word in what must have seemed like a very long minute.

"Sure, we'll help you," I said. "That's a really nice idea."

Jeff relaxed, smiled, and gave me a hug. "Thanks, Katie. This means a lot to me. I know how special your mom is to you. And I hope you know how special both of you are to me, too."

I felt my eyes fill with tears then, and the last thing I wanted to do was cry. I had been doing enough of that lately.

"Come on! Let's tell everyone," I said, and we went back into the dining room.

My friends had been talking, but they stopped as soon as we walked in. I looked at Jeff.

"So, I am going to ask Katie's mom to marry me," he said. "And I would like to present the ring to her on a special cupcake. Like a proposal cupcake. And I thought you would be able to help me with that."

"I knew it!" cried Alexis.

"Ooh, a wedding!" Emma said, her blue eyes shining. "Katie, your mom has to come to The Special Day bridal shop for her dress. I know Mona has the perfect one for her."

"And I could design your bridesmaid's dress!" added Mia. "You're going to be a bridesmaid, right?"

"Hey, Jeff hasn't even proposed to her yet," I said, laughing. "She might say no."

"Not a chance," Alexis retorted.

"Well, you'd better design a spectacular cupcake for me, to make sure," said Jeff.

"This is so on trend," said Alexis. She whipped out her phone. "Wait, I bookmarked a whole Pinterest page of proposal cupcakes. There are so many awesome things we can do."

"I think we need a classic flavor," said Emma. "We don't want the cupcake to take away from the proposal."

"I'm thinking lots of tiny fondant flowers," Mia said with a dreamy look in her eyes.

Alexis turned to Jeff. "Before we start brainstorming, we need to get your order filled out. When do you want this done?"

Everyone starting chatting at once, excited, but my mind was spinning with noncupcake thoughts. I was happy for Mom. I thought I would be okay with having Jeff for a stepdad, but I wasn't completely sure. Here I was, about to get a stepdad, and I didn't even know my real dad.

That's when I knew for sure that I was going to take the internship. It was time for me to find out who Marc Donald Brown really was—and if he really was ready to be my dad.

## CHAPTER 8

## I'm an Intern!

It was pretty cool that Jeff brought in the Cupcake Club and me on his surprise proposal to my mom. But that meant I had to keep the surprise a secret from her! It wasn't easy. I was glad I had the internship thing to distract me.

When I got back home from the Cupcake Club meeting, I had told Mom that I was going to accept Marc Donald Brown's offer. She said I could e-mail him, so I did, and he got right back to me.

> That's great, Katie! I know I said you could work Saturday mornings, but I know there's no school this Friday. Would you like to come in on Friday morning? That's when Melissa comes in to prepare the desserts in advance.

At first I wondered how he knew about the school schedule, but then I remembered that his daughters went to school in the next town. That would explain it. Everybody in New Jersey had Friday off so the teachers could all go to some convention. I didn't have any plans.

I typed back.

I can do Friday. What time?

He must have been online because he replied straightaway.

How does 8–12 sound?

I responded just as quickly.

I'll ask Mom.

Mom said okay, and Marc Donald Brown and I e-mailed back and forth about how it was going to work. I had to wear comfortable shoes with nonslip soles, and Mom took me out and bought me a pair of these canvas clogs with thick rubber bottoms that she knew about because her dental assistants wear them. And Marc Donald Brown said it was okay to wear jeans and told me to pull back my hair.

By Thursday night I was a nervous wreck. I had spent the whole week (1) trying not to accidentally mention to Mom that I knew Jeff was going to propose and (2) worrying about what my first day as a pastry chef intern would be like in Marc Donald Brown's restaurant.

I carefully set out my outfit for the next day: my new shoes (which I had been wearing every night to break them in), my best pair of jeans (no rips or pen drawings), and a plain black T-shirt (because I remembered that everyone who worked in the restaurant wore black). I set my alarm for six a.m. because I wanted plenty of time to get ready.

The alarm rang as scheduled on Friday morning, and I hit snooze twice (because I am still me, after all), but I had time to wash up. Mom and I left the house at seven thirty and got to the restaurant by seven forty-five.

"Oh no! We're early!" I said as we pulled into a space in front of Chez Donald.

"That's good," Mom said. "It's your first day of work. It shows that you're responsible."

"Oh," I said, nodding. That made sense. *Good to know,* I thought.

Mom walked inside with me. The restaurant looked just like it did the time that Mia and I had tried to eat lunch there. It was a wide, bright space with shiny dark wood floors. The walls were pale yellow on top, with dark wood on the bottom half. The tables were set with crisp white tablecloths and gleaming glasses.

Marc Donald Brown was standing at the hostess's stand, going through a pile of receipts. He looked up and smiled when we came in.

"Good morning," he said. "Katie, I'm so glad you're doing this."

"Yeah," I said.

Mom handed him her business card. "This is my work number, in case you don't have it handy. I'll be at the office this morning, but I will be here at noon to pick her up."

"Great, great," MDB said, running a hand through his hair. "You should meet Melissa before you go, Sharon. Follow me."

He led us into the restaurant's kitchen, and I couldn't help feeling excited. Restaurant kitchens have always seemed like special places to me—it's where the magic happens, and customers can't go there normally. The Chez Donald kitchen was absolutely spotless. A bank of cooktops lined one wall, and in the center of the room were two rows of shiny stainless-steel workstations. Tucked underneath the stations were all kinds of pots, pans, and mixing bowls. I started to feel excited. I wanted to cook with every one of them!

There were a few workers in white shirts and pants, busy chopping vegetables. MDB led us through the kitchen to a plump woman slicing apples. She wore a black chef's coat, and her brown hair was pulled back into a bun.

"Melissa, this is my daughter Katie I was telling you about," Marc Donald Brown said.

Melissa put down her knife. "Katie, the intern? I don't think you told me she was your daughter. But I thought your girls were all little?"

The awkwardness had begun! I looked at Mom, who was biting her lower lip.

"Katie is my daughter from Sharon, my first wife," he said, pointing to Mom. "Katie lives in Maple Grove, and she's already a great baker."

A light went on in Melissa's blue eyes. "Oh right, Katie! Nice to meet you!" she said. She came out from behind the table and pumped my hand. Then she shook Mom's hand.

"Don has said many nice things about you, and Katie is eager to learn," Mom said.

"Great!" Melissa said. "I can definitely use an extra pair of hands."

Mom looked at me. "I'll see you soon, Katie. You'll do great." Then she hugged me.

"Thanks," I said, and she said good-bye to MDB and Melissa and then walked out of the kitchen.

Marc Donald Brown ran his hand through his hair again. "Well, I've got to go do some orders, so I'll let you two get at it," he said, and then he ambled away.

Melissa went over to a wall and pulled off a black apron.

"You can wear this," she said. "We're going to get our hands dirty this morning."

"Great!" I said. That's one thing I liked about baking—cracking eggs, getting my hands in dough, stuff like that. It's like playing, but you get something delicious to eat when you're done.

"I'll start by showing you around," Melissa said, and she pointed to her workstation. "This is the pastry station. I do all my prep here. In the morning, I make all the desserts, and I'm here through the lunch shift. At night there's a sous chef who plates the desserts and does any finishing touches, like adding whipped cream or heating things up."

I nodded. "I read Sonya Beck's memoir about being a pastry chef, and that's how she explained it too," I said.

Melissa raised an eyebrow. "Wow, did you read that after you got the internship?"

"No, I read that last year for fun," I replied.

She grinned. "A girl after my own heart," she said. "Okay, let me show you the walk-in."

She led me to a large, walk-in refrigerator. It was lined with shelves loaded with vegetables, fruit, meat, and more, and everything was labeled and dated.

"This is where the cold stuff is," she said. "So if I ask you to grab me butter or milk or strawberries, you'll find them in here."

She grabbed a large plastic container labeled BLACKBERRY COMPOTE and then led me out of the walk-in and into the room next door.

"Here's the pantry," she said.

Once again, my eyes went wide. Mom and I had a tiny pantry off the kitchen, but it was nothing like this. The pantry, too, held rows of steel shelves, filled with neatly labeled ingredients. There were bags of beans and grains, bins of flour and sugar, and what looked like hundreds of spices.

"You could get lost in here," I said.

Melissa laughed. "And you just might," she said. She pointed to one shelf. "My baking stuff is all in one area, so it shouldn't be too hard to find."

After that she led me to a sink. "Wash your hands and then put on a pair of gloves from that box," she said. "I need you to fill some tart shells for me."

I did as instructed, and Melissa put the container of compote on her station. She disappeared into the pantry and came back with a large metal tray of small tart shells.

"We had some amazing blackberries come in yesterday, so I immediately thought of tarts," she said. "I'm leaning toward a tart trio—a mini blackberry tart, an apple tart, and maybe a chocolate tart."

Just hearing the description made me want to drool.

"I baked some tart shells this morning," she said. "If you can fill each tart with the blackberry compote, that would be great. There are two more trays in the pantry, so keep going when you finish this one. I'm going to work on the apple tarts."

"How much compote should I put in each tart?" I asked her.

She opened the container and picked up a small scoop—almost like an ice-cream scoop but smaller. I had one like it at home that I used to scoop out cookie dough. It helped you get evenly sized portions.

"Just before the tippy-top," she said, demonstrating for me. "Leave a little bit of room at the rim. Got it?"

"Got it," I said, and then I got to work. I started off slowly, because I didn't want to mess them up. The tart shells were kind of delicate, and I kept worrying that I would crush one every time I picked one up.

I got through the first eight okay. Then when I did the ninth one, some of the compote spilled onto the side of the tart.

"Um, Melissa?" I asked.

Melissa looked up from her apples. "What's up?"

"I spilled some of the blackberry onto the side of the tart with this one," I told her. I could feel my face getting hot. What a rookie mistake!

"No biggie," she said. She picked it up and used a clean cloth to wipe away the stray blackberry filling. "See? Good as new. And if it wasn't . . ."

She popped the tart into her mouth. "Just eat the evidence."

I laughed, relieved that Melissa wasn't angry or upset or anything. Then I got back to work.

Soon, I fell into a rhythm. I had a lot of tarts to fill. I must have been really focused because when I had finished, I saw Melissa was rolling out some dough. I hadn't even seen her make it!

"I think I'm done," I announced.

Melissa walked over to me. "Nice job." Then she frowned. "But these are kinda plain. And they could be prettier. Have you ever made a simple syrup before?"

I nodded. "We learned at my summer cooking camp. Equal parts water and sugar, simmered together."

"So, can you make me a cup? I'm thinking some candied almond slices would be nice. And maybe some tiny sprigs of mint," she said.

"Blackberry and mint are awesome together," I told her. "I made a sorbet like that once."

Melissa grinned. "I'd better watch out, or you'll be taking my job," she said, and I blushed. "Now, go make that syrup for me."

I stared at the kitchen for a minute, suddenly nervous again. I wasn't just filling tarts—I was cooking! Sure, I mean, it was only simple syrup, but still.

*Think, Katie, think,* I told myself. *You need a measuring cup for liquids, and a measuring cup for dry ingredients, and a small saucepan to make the syrup. . . .*

Melissa was humming to herself as she cut her dough into little circles. She must have had a lot of faith in me, I guessed, because she didn't seem worried that I would mess things up. I didn't want to let her down.

First, I went to the pantry to get the sugar. I was coming back out when I bumped into Marc Donald Brown.

"Oh, hey, Katie," he said. "Is Melissa keeping you busy?"

"Yeah," I replied. "We're, um, making tarts."

"No cupcakes?" MDB asked me.

"Well, I guess they're not on the menu," I said. "So, um, I should get to the stove."

"Sure, sure," he said, and then he hurried off.

I found what I needed, and pretty soon, I had the syrup gently simmering on the stove. It didn't take long to make. Just as I took the syrup off the heat, Melissa came by with a measuring cup full of almonds and dumped it into the saucepan.

"Now, give them a good stir," she said. "And spread them out on that baking sheet over there."

The baking sheet was covered with a mat made of silicone—I had one of those at home, too. It was nonstick, and besides baking, it was good for when you were making sticky stuff, like peanut brittle.

While the almonds cooled, Melissa had me wash and dry a bunch of mint and then pick off the leaves. It was kind of painstaking, but Melissa started talking to me while we worked.

"So, what did your dad say back there about cupcakes?" she asked.

"My friends and I own a cupcake business, the Cupcake Club," I replied.

Melissa's eyebrows rose. "The Cupcake Club? That's you? I had one of your cupcakes at a bridal shower this summer. Pineapple coconut. It was awesome."

"Thanks!" I said. "Usually, I come up with the flavors, but that one was my friend Mia's idea. The mother of the bride had a whole tropical theme going."

"So what's your next gig?" she asked.

I decided not to tell her about the proposal cupcake—that would be complicated.

"We're baking cupcakes for this magazine launch," I answered. "They want us to do a cupcake that follows the latest trends. My friend Alexis researched it and says it's vegetables in cupcakes. It sounds interesting, but I'm not so sure."

Melissa looked thoughtful. "Well, the obvious would be, like, a sweet potato cupcake with brown sugar frosting. But if you wanted to be really adventurous, you could do a zucchini cupcake or something like that. With avocado buttercream."

I made a face. "Avocado buttercream?"

Melissa nodded. "It's a vegan thing, I guess. But there are a lot of recipes out there. It's surprisingly good."

I was having a tough time imagining what an avocado frosting would taste like, but I was definitely intrigued.

"Thanks," I said. "It's worth trying out. We do test baking sessions all the time."

"You sound so professional," Melissa said. "Your dad must be really proud of you."

"Yeah, well, he doesn't exactly know me very well." The words just kind of came out by themselves. I barely knew Melissa. Why was I telling her this?

Thankfully, Melissa was cool about it. She just nodded, and then she changed the subject.

"Okay, let's start dressing these babies," she said.

We worked together at first, topping each mini tart with two slivers of candied almond and one mint leaf. Then, when I got the hang of it, Melissa went back to finish her apple tarts. She also had an ice cream going, and a chocolate cake in the oven. I don't know how she got it all done so fast!

When the tarts were done, I stared at the trays with rows and rows of perfect little treats. It was a good feeling—the same feeling I get when I look at rows of perfect cupcakes. But this time I was baking in a professional kitchen!

After that, Melissa had me help out with a bunch of different stuff. I was grating some dark chocolate when Marc Donald Brown walked back in.

"How's it going?" he asked.

"Great!" Melissa said. "She's a real winner, Don."

"Glad to hear that," he said. Then he turned to me. "Katie, your mom will be here in about five minutes. I'll walk you outside."

"Already?" I asked. I couldn't believe that the whole morning had passed so quickly.

"Before you take her from me, I need to let her taste one of the tarts she helped me with," Melissa said. She picked up a mini tart and handed it to me. "What do you think?"

The crust was buttery, the blackberries were sweet, the almond slivers were crunchy, and the mint brightened it all up.

"Delicious," I said after I had finished. "Thanks, Melissa."

"See you soon, Katie!" she said.

Then I walked outside the restaurant with MDB.

"I'm glad you had a good morning, Katie," he told me.

"Thanks," I said. "Thanks for giving me the internship. I really like it so far."

Marc Donald Brown smiled. "So, I'd really like for you to meet your sisters soon," he said. "What do you think?"

I was still kind of nervous about the idea. But I had been nervous about the internship, too, and the morning had been great. Not awkward at all. (Of course, I had barely seen MDB the whole morning, so maybe that was why.)

Still, it was worth a try.

"Sure," I said.

He looked relieved. "Great!" he said. "I'll e-mail your mother to set up a date."

"Okay, thanks," I said, and then I saw Mom's car pull up. "See you soon."

I ran out to the car.

"How did it go?" Mom asked when I got into the car.

I licked my lips. I could still taste the blackberry. The tarts were delicious. Melissa was supernice. And Marc Donald Brown was just . . . just fine.

"Pretty sweet, I guess," I said, and I meant it.

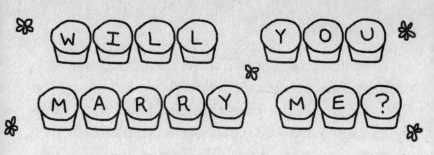

## CHAPTER 9

## Some Interesting Proposals

The rest of the weekend was really busy! I'd texted the girls earlier about testing one of Melissa's suggestions for cupcakes, and they agreed to give it a try. I had to do homework on Saturday afternoon, and then after dinner, Mom took me shopping for ingredients for our cupcake baking session the next day. I knew I needed sweet potatoes, brown sugar, zucchini, and . . .

"Avocados? Really?" Mom asked as I put them into the basket.

"Well, it was Melissa's idea," I said. "I looked it up. Even chef Alton Brown has a recipe for avocado buttercream. So it must be kind of good, right? Anyway, that's why we're testing the recipe. So we can decide."

Mom shook her head. "Well, I'll be curious to know how the vote turns out!"

I paid for the groceries with funds from the Cupcake Club and saved my receipt to give to Alexis. She kept track of all our expenses and profits. Most of the time we always had a profit, and when we did, we split it four ways.

"Oh, by the way, we're going out for pizza with Jeff tonight," Mom said. "He's got Emily with him. Her mom's on a business trip."

"Oh, okay," I said. Emily is pretty nice, just like her dad. She's a couple of years younger than I am, and she thinks the Cupcake Club is cool.

We stopped off at home, put away the groceries, and then headed to Vinnie's Pizza in town. We could smell the pizza a block away. They make the best pizza there!

We got there first, and Mom asked for a table for four. Sally, our server, gave us a big smile.

"The usual for you guys?" she asked.

Mom, Jeff, Emily, and I had a sort of tradition every time we went to Vinnie's. We always ordered the same thing: two veggie pizzas, one order of garlic knots, and one order of chicken fingers.

"Sounds good," Mom said, and we slid into a booth.

"I'm so hungry!" I said.

Jeff and Emily walked in. Emily has long brown hair and brown eyes—like me. I wondered: Did people think we were a family when we all sat together? That Emily and I were sisters? And then I wondered—did Emily know what her dad was planning?

I didn't have to wait long to find out. Mom got up to hug Jeff and then went to the restroom. I shot Jeff a look.

"Yes, Emily knows," he said. "In fact, I'm going to bring her to your Cupcake Club meeting tomorrow night if that's okay. She wants to help choose the cupcake design."

"A cupcake proposal is so cute!" said Emily. And then she added, shyly, "I was wondering, maybe I could help you bake them?"

"Sure, if you're around on baking day," I said. "But that depends on the proposal day. When's the big night?"

Jeff shook his head subtly, and Mom walked back up at that moment and sat down.

"We went ahead and ordered our usual," she said. "Hope that's okay."

"Of course," said Jeff, and just then Sally came by with our drinks.

It was a pretty fun night. Emily and Jeff both had a lot of questions about what it was like to work in a restaurant kitchen. When we were done eating, Jeff and Emily walked Mom and me to our car.

This is going to be different really soon, I realized. Soon, we'd all be coming to the restaurant in *our* car—and then all going back to *our* house.

Then it hit me—where was Emily going to sleep when she spent weekends with us? We only have two bedrooms in the house. I was dying to ask Mom about it, but I didn't want her to get suspicious. I'd have to worry about that later.

On Sunday, I went to Alexis's house for a Cupcake Club meeting and baking session. Mia, Emma, Alexis, and I gathered in Alexis's neat, sparkling kitchen. I started to unpack my bags of supplies.

"So, Melissa at the restaurant suggested sweet potato cupcakes with brown sugar icing or zucchini cupcakes with avocado buttercream," I said. "I found recipes for both. And last night, I cooked the sweet potatoes and puréed them to save time today." I held up a container to show them.

"Sweet potato sounds okay," said Emma. "At least it's got the word 'sweet' in it. But avocado frosting?"

"Well, Alexis said we needed to be trendy," I said. "And that stuff is pretty trendy."

"It's worth a try," Alexis said. "Let's get started on the first batter. Mia, you're still working on the proposal cupcake proposal, right?"

"That's a lot of 'proposals.'" I giggled.

Mia grinned. "Yes, I am working on the proposal proposal. Mind if I print out some stuff, or do you need me to help bake?"

"No, that's fine," Alexis said. "Mr. Green will be here in about an hour."

Alexis, Emma, and I tied on our aprons (we all have matching aprons, with our Cupcake Club logo on them) and got to work. Even when we bake different flavors, the process is the same. We cream the sugar, eggs, and butter together in one mixer. In another bowl we mix the dry ingredients. Then we mix additional wet ingredients into the sugar mixture (like sweet potato purée or flavorings, like vanilla) and then slowly mix in the dry ingredients. The sweet potato cupcakes had yummy stuff like cinnamon and nutmeg added too.

While the sweet potato cupcakes baked, we washed out the bowls. Emma made the brown sugar frosting, and I started grating zucchini for the zucchini cupcakes. The recipe called for cinnamon, as well as cocoa powder and even some chocolate chips.

"That doesn't look half bad," Emma said, peering into the mixing bowl. "It might even be tasty with chocolate frosting."

I got the zucchini cupcakes into the oven, just as the sweet potato cupcakes came out. Then I started to make the avocado buttercream. It was pretty simple: avocado, powdered sugar, and lemon juice.

I dipped a spoon into the bowl to taste it.

"Creamy," I reported. "And lemony. It doesn't even taste like avocado. You should try it, Emma."

"No, thanks!" Emma said.

Then it was time to frost the cooled-off sweet potato cupcakes. Alexis and I used small flat icing spatulas to get a nice, smooth look.

"So, how was working in your dad's restaurant?" she asked me.

"It was fun," I said. "Melissa the pastry chef is nice, and I didn't even really see my dad."

"That's good," Mia said, looking up from her laptop. "I'm glad it wasn't weird."

"Me too," I agreed.

Alexis and I quickly finished frosting the sweet potato cupcakes, and then we cleaned up as much as we could and frosted the zucchini cupcakes when they were cooled off. Mia had finished printing out the proposal and had placed it neatly in a pink file folder with our logo on it. She looked at the zucchini cupcakes and frowned.

"Well, I don't know how they taste, but they sure don't look pretty," she said.

"Can you jazz them up?" I asked.

"I've got to think about it," Mia replied. "Bright green cupcakes are great for a kid's party but not a sophisticated magazine launch."

Just then the doorbell rang. Alexis answered it and walked back into the kitchen with Jeff and Emily.

"Hey, girls," he said. "I think you all know Emily."

"We sure do," said Emma. "Hi, Emily!"

"Hi," Emily said in that cute shy way of hers.

"We're excited to see your proposal for my proposal," he said, and Alexis and I both laughed. We had made the same joke! "I think it's going to happen next Sunday. Does that work?"

"Should be fine," said Alexis. "The *Relish New Jersey* party is the day before."

"And my dad is bringing me back early for the magazine launch, so if we make your cupcakes on Saturday night, I'll be able to work on them too," Mia said.

"Great!" said Jeff. "What have you got?"

Mia opened her folder. "Well, there are two popular ways to do a proposal cupcake," she said. "The first way is to do a single cupcake in a fancy gift box. Then when Mrs. Brown opens the box, she'll find a cupcake with the engagement ring stuck in the frosting."

She passed some printouts of gift-boxed cupcakes to Jeff and Emily.

"The second way is to do a whole platter with a message on it, like this one," Mia said, passing him another printout. "See? There are sixteen cupcakes, and they spell out, 'Will You Marry Me?'"

I looked at the image. It was pretty cute. The message was spelled out with one letter written in icing on each cupcake. The extra cupcakes had pretty flowers piped on them.

"I like this," Jeff said.

"Me too," Emily and I said at the same time.

"Great!" said Alexis. "Now you just need to pick out some flavors and colors."

"Well, I was thinking green and brown," Jeff said. "You know, because . . ."

I slapped my forehead. "Mr. Green and Mrs. Brown! I get it. That's pretty cool."

"Ooh, that's nice," said Emma. "I can picture

those colors at a woodland-themed wedding. Moss green and soft brown."

Mia took out her sketchbook and started sketching. "We could do brown flowers with green leaves, and maybe add some cute fondant toadstools—you know, red with white spots."

"And green and brown letters?" I asked. "Then what color would the frosting be?"

"White, I think," Mia said.

"We could do vanilla icing or cream cheese icing or marshmallow icing," I said. "Mom likes all those."

"What about chocolate cupcakes, so the cupcakes are brown? And the lettering could be green?" Emma suggested.

I frowned. "Chocolate is good, but it's not special."

"What about mocha?" Alexis asked.

"That would be nice," Jeff said. "Sharon likes her coffee."

"And maybe we could do an icing with real vanilla bean, to be extra special," I suggested.

"Yes!" agreed Emma.

Mia kept sketching, and pretty soon, we had an awesome proposal proposal put together.

"I love it," Jeff said. "Perfect. I knew this was a good idea."

"So, what's *your* proposal proposal?" I asked. "How are you going to do it?"

Jeff grinned. "I'd like to keep that a secret from you and Emily, if you don't mind. I want there to be some element of surprise for you two. I'll confirm the arrangement and payment with Alexis."

"No problem!" Alexis said.

I looked at the clock. "You guys should be going," I told Jeff and Emily. "Mom is coming to pick me up soon. She's going to wonder what you're doing here."

"No problem," Jeff said. "Thanks again for doing this. It's going to be really special."

Jeff and Emily said good-bye and left.

"It's sweet that he brought Emily here," Emma said. "This must be weird for her, too."

I hadn't thought about that before, but I knew Emma was right. Emily was used to having alone time with her dad, just like I had my mom all to myself.

"She seems pretty cool with it," I said.

"She does," said Mia. "But she might be holding some feelings inside."

"I guess I could talk to her about it," I said, and then I remembered something. "Hey, we should taste those cupcakes before it's time to go."

80

We cut one cupcake of each flavor into fourths and tasted each one.

"The sweet potato is delicious," Alexis said. "But I'm not sure how sophisticated it is."

"Well, I actually think the zucchini and avocado is pretty tasty," Mia said. "I could work on a way to make them look nicer."

"I have to admit, the avocado isn't as bad as I thought," Emma chimed in. "But I don't think we should tell people it's avocado. They might not eat it. It might not sound like a yummy ingredient."

"Well, we don't have much time to figure it out," Alexis said. "We'll need to bake Friday night for Saturday."

"I think we can do it at my house," I offered.

"Let me think on designs for the avocado cupcake," Mia said. "I just need to sleep on it. We can talk at school tomorrow."

"Sounds good," Alexis said, and at that moment, my cell phone beeped. It was my mom.

"I've got to go," I said.

Alexis put a paper plate with green cupcakes on it into my hands. "Take some with you, please."

"I'll take some too," Mia said. "Eddie will eat just about anything we bake."

I got my stuff together and went out to the car.

"Wow, are those the avocado cupcakes?" Mom asked when she noticed the plate of goodies as I got into the car. "They're very green."

"You've got to try one when we get home," I said. "They're not bad."

Mom pulled away from Alexis's house. "So, I got a phone call from your dad. His restaurant is closed on Mondays, and he thought you might want to meet your half sisters after school."

"Tomorrow?" I asked, and my voice came out like a squeak. "Wow, that's soon!"

"Do you want to wait?" Mom asked.

I thought about it. It did feel soon—but things were moving pretty fast these days. I figured I might as well get it over with it.

"You can tell him I'll do it," I said, and those familiar feelings of worry came sweeping in like a tidal wave.

What if my sisters didn't like me? What if I didn't like them?

Marc Donald Brown's proposal that I meet my half sisters was one proposal I wasn't sure I was ready for! I always thought I wanted to be part of a bigger family—but this was too much too fast!

# CHAPTER 10

## Daddy's Girls

$\mathcal{M}$arc Donald Brown had suggested to Mom that I meet his family in his restaurant. It would be quiet and private there. I was kind of glad he hadn't wanted me to go to his house, so I was cool with that. Mom said she'd pick me up after school and bring me there.

I was thinking about my three half sisters as I rode the bus to school Monday morning with Mia. My thoughts were interrupted when my friend George Martinez peered over the back of the seat.

"Hey, Katie, want to go to the park after school?" he asked.

George and I are friends, but we're friends who *like* like each other. We're not dating, but we hang out a lot, and if there's a school dance or something like that, George always asks me to go with him.

I'd been busy lately with Cupcake meetings and Marc Donald Brown and my cold, so I hadn't hung out with him in a while.

"I wish I could," I said. "I actually have to go see my dad tonight. And meet my half sisters."

George was a good listener, so he knew my whole abandoned-by-dad situation. He got a surprised look on his face when I told him what had been going on with me lately.

"Wow, so that's happening?" he asked after I'd finished updating him, and I nodded.

"Yup," I said. "This morning I'm an only child. This afternoon I'll be the big sister to three little girls."

"I wonder if they'll have silly arms like you?" George teased. "Silly Arms" is his nickname for me, because of the way I play volleyball in gym. (And yes, the name pretty much describes what I look like on the court.)

I laughed. "Oh man, I hope not!"

George punched me in the shoulder. "You'll make a great big sister. Don't worry, Katie." Then he ducked back into his seat.

It was nice for George to say that. He's a big brother, so he knows what it means to be an older sibling. But to be honest, I was worried about being a big sister—to Emily as well as to my half sisters. I had been an only child all these years. This was a lot of change all at once.

Mia caught my worried expression. "Don't worry, Katie," she said. "They'll love you. And if they don't, then they don't deserve you."

"Thanks, Mia," I said.

"So, I have some ideas for the zucchini-avocado cupcake," she said. "I can't wait to show you guys at lunchtime."

"Cool! I can't wait to see them," I said. It was a relief to think about cupcakes instead of my crazy life for a change!

Later on, after we were all settled in the cafeteria, Alexis told us she had heard back from the people at *Relish New Jersey* magazine. They told her they loved the idea of zucchini cupcakes.

Then Mia showed us her design ideas. "I thought about going graphic, with black polka dots made out of fondant," she said, showing us a sketch. "But we all know that fondant isn't supertasty, so a lot of it might not work."

I nodded.

"Then I thought about the name of the magazine," Mia said. "*Relish New Jersey.* Relish is green, right? So maybe we could do the *R* from their logo in red? Because relish has pieces of red stuff in it?"

"Peppers," I said.

"That's brilliant," said Alexis, "using their logo. And you're right: The green works for this party. Hey, I think we're good. What do you think, Emma?"

Emma frowned. "I think it's risky. This is a big launch. People want delicious more than trendy."

"They *think* that's what they want," said Alexis. "But what they really want is to follow the trends, trust me."

Emma shrugged. "If you guys all want to do it, I'm in."

To be honest, I thought Emma had a point. But I was so preoccupied with the whole new-family thing that I wasn't too invested in the cupcakes.

"I'll get the ingredients for the baking session," I said. "Six dozen, right?"

Alexis nodded. "Yes. This is going to be great. We're going to get lots of exposure."

"I just hope it's good," Emma muttered softly.

The rest of the day went by quickly, and I almost jumped when the final bell rang. When I got outside, Mom was waiting for me. As I got into the car, I realized that she was probably taking off work to do this for me. In fact, she had been doing that a lot lately. I climbed into the seat and gave her an awkward hug over her seat belt.

"What's that for?" Mom asked.

"Thanks for taking me," I said.

We arrived at Chez Donald a few minutes later, and this time we had to knock on the door to be let in. Marc Donald Brown unlocked it for us.

"Katie, Sharon, come in," he said.

His wife and three daughters were sitting around one of the tables, drinking what looked like cocoa out of the restaurant mugs. The littlest blond girl was sitting in her mother's lap, playing with Jasmine's blond braid.

Mom put her arm around me, and I was glad, because right now things felt super extra weird. Those little blond girls were my sisters!

Mom walked with me to the table.

"You must be Jasmine," she said to MDB's wife. "I'm Sharon. And this is Katie, of course."

Jasmine smiled nervously and shifted her daughter so she could shake Mom's hand. I noticed that her blond hair was coming loose from her braid, and she wasn't wearing makeup. She didn't look like a supergirlie exotic "Jasmine" like I was expecting. More like a . . . I don't know. A Sarah or a Becca.

"Nice to meet you," she said. "This one on my lap is Riley," she said. "And my oldest over there is Cecile; next to her is Ella."

"Hi, Katie!" Cecile said, practically shouting, while Ella squirmed and ducked under the table.

Mom looked at me. "I'll be close by. Text me when you're done."

I nodded, and as she left, I got a lump in my throat. I was alone in a room of strangers! But they were my family. It was so confusing.

"Have a seat, Katie," MDB said. When I did, he put a mug in front of me. "I made us some cocoa. And Melissa made us some cookies."

"Thanks," I said. I gripped the mug and inhaled the scent of warm chocolate. They say that chocolate can activate parts of your brain that make you feel happy or something like that. I hoped it would work.

I wasn't really sure what to say—but Cecile solved that problem for me.

"Katie, my dad says you go to school in Maple Grove," she said. "Is it nice there? Are your teachers nice? My teacher this year is Ms. Ross, and she's really nice, which is good because last year I had Ms. O'Brien, and she wasn't nice. She yelled all the time for no reason."

I smiled. Cecile was talking really fast and practically bouncing in her seat. And she was loud, too, and she had spilled cocoa on her shirt—nothing like the perfect, neat little blond sister I had imagined.

"The middle school teachers are all really nice," I told her.

Ella emerged from under the table. "I like your sneakers," she said.

"Thanks," I replied. Then I took a look at her sneakers. She had on pink ones, the kind that light up when you take a step. "I like yours too."

Riley stopped squirming and thrust her foot out at me so I could admire *her* sneaker next.

"Hey, yours is purple, just like mine," I told her. "But yours is sparkly. Cool."

Riley smiled and then buried her face in her mom's hair.

I had to admit—all three of them were pretty cute.

"Katie, it's so nice that you came to meet us," Jasmine said. "The girls have been so excited to meet their big sister."

"Yeah, and I don't even mind not being the big sister anymore because I can still be a big sister to Ella and Riley, but then I can have you as a big sister too," Cecile said, all in one breath.

"Well, that's good," I said. "Maybe you can give me some tips about being a big sister. Because I've never been one until now."

"Oh, I can give you lots of tips," Cecile said. Then she stopped to take a breath, and her mom jumped in.

"Katie, Don tells me that you and your friends have a cupcake business," she said. "That sounds like a lot of fun, but also a lot of work, too."

I nodded. "It gets tough when I run track in the spring," I said. "But we do a lot on weekends, so that works out."

"Who are your clients usually?" Jasmine asked.

"Well, friends and family, of course, but we do a lot of advertising, so we get all kinds of jobs," I said. "Like birthday parties and baby showers. This weekend we're doing cupcakes for the launch party of *Relish New Jersey* magazine."

"I think I got an invitation to that," said MDB, joining the conversation for the first time.

"You should come!" I blurted out. "Then you'd get to see the Cupcake Club in action."

"Yes, that would be nice," Jasmine chimed in, and I swear she gave my dad a look, like a warning look. I wasn't sure why, though.

"Sure, sure, I'll go," my dad said. And yes, I was starting to think of him as my dad. It was getting hard not to. Besides, my dad was going to come see the Cupcake Club! That was pretty cool.

"Daddy, can you take us bowling this weekend?" Cecile asked. "That was so fun when we went last time. Ella made more strikes than anybody, and she didn't even put her fingers in the ball like you're supposed to."

Ella started laughing. "Daddy threw so many gutter balls!"

"Remember when we went to the museum with the big dinosaurs, and Daddy ran away like he was scared?" Cecile asked.

Ella put her arms in front of her and started making dinosaur noises.

Then Riley climbed out of Jasmine's arms and went to Marc Donald Brown. She held out her arms.

"Daddy!"

MDB picked her up and rocked back and forth in his chair, hugging her.

*Daddy! Daddy! Daddy!*

That was when my ears starting to ring, and my stomach dropped, and I felt like the whole world around me had frozen. Yes, Marc Donald Brown was my "dad." But he wasn't my "daddy." I had never gone bowling with him. Or to a museum. I didn't have any funny memories of him. And he had never held me in his arms and rocked me, as far as I could remember.

The girls were all talking and laughing, so I didn't think anybody noticed how pale and sweaty I was getting. Then Jasmine did.

"Katie, are you okay?" she asked.

"Oh, yeah," I said. "I just . . . I have a lot of homework. I should text my mom."

Cecile jumped around in her seat to face me. "Ms. Ross is nice, but she gives us too much homework! I have four math pages tonight and two spelling pages."

"Wow, that's a lot," I said, typing my message to Mom.

Come now, please, I wrote.

On my way, she responded.

"What's your favorite subject, Katie?" Cecile asked. "Mine's science. Is yours science too?"

"Science is good," I said. "But I like history more."

Cecile's chatter was helping. I could just nod and answer questions and not really think.

Luckily, Mom arrived at the door a minute later.

She must have been hovering around, like she'd done last time.

"Gotta go," I said. "It was, uh, it was good meeting you."

Then I hurried out of there.

# CHAPTER 11

## Emotional Avalanche!

When I got into the car, Mom didn't ask me how things went. She could probably tell from the look on my face that I didn't feel like talking—she was good at that. She turned on the radio, and I gazed out the window.

When we got home, I ran upstairs and flopped down onto my bed, and then I cried. I mean, *cried*. My tears soaked my pillowcase, and I kept making this horrible hiccupping noise, but I just couldn't stop.

After a few minutes the sobs slowed to sniffles, and I rolled over onto my back and stared at the ceiling. I could feel some stray snot trickling out of my nose. Gross!

I was blowing my nose when Mom knocked on the door.

"Come in," I croaked.

Mom sat down on the bed and put her arm around me. "Poor Katie. This is quite a lot for you, isn't it?"

I nodded.

"I'm sorry it didn't go well," Mom said.

"It was okay," I said. "I mean, Jasmine was nice and my half sisters are cute. But then they started calling Dad 'Daddy' and talking about stuff they did together, and . . . I never did any of those things with him. And he might be my 'father,' but he'll never be my 'daddy.'"

Mom squeezed me hard. "Oh, Katie, that must hurt a lot," she said.

I started to cry again. "It does," I said, my voice tight.

"You dad hasn't been there for you," she said. "But he wants to be here for you now. And whatever that looks like is up to you, Katie. You can see him as much or as little as you want. I'll still love you, and I'll always be here for you."

*Will you?* I wondered, thinking about Jeff's upcoming proposal. But I didn't say anything. I wasn't going to spoil that surprise, no matter how bad I was feeling.

"And it might take time with your dad," Mom

went on. "It's not easy to build a whole relationship in just a few days. You and I have had a lot longer than that!"

"I guess that makes sense," I said. "And I mean, I think I would like to see my half sisters again. I just don't know if I can do it again soon."

"Take all the time you need," Mom said, and then she got up. "I'm going to go start dinner."

I flopped back down again and stared at my ceiling for a long time. After a while my thoughts drifted to cupcakes. I'd have to make a shopping list for both the magazine launch cupcakes and the proposal cupcakes, and I'd have to get Mom to take me shopping before Friday. . . .

I sat up, went to my desk, and started writing in the notebook that I use for Cupcake stuff. (It has a cupcake on the cover, of course.) My throat was scratchy, but at least I wasn't crying anymore.

As I worked on the shopping list, I had a thought that I'd had many times before: Thank goodness for the Cupcake Club!

I only heard from Marc Donald Brown once more that week, asking me if I wanted to work at the restaurant on Saturday morning. I knew it was going to be a busy day because we had the magazine launch in the afternoon, but since we were baking the night before, I thought I could do it, so I said yes. I was looking forward to working with Melissa again, even if I was still feeling weird about my dad.

Mom took me out shopping on Thursday night, and on Friday after school, I started getting ready. I chopped up veggies for a vegetarian chili, and Mom helped me cook it when she got back from work. Since we had a lot of baking to do, Emma and Alexis were going to come over on the early side, around six. We could eat chili with cheese and corn chips while we baked. Sometimes we would get pizza, but lately, I had been craving some chili.

The finished pot of chili was simmering on the stove when Alexis and Emma came to the door. The bowls, spoons, and extras were set up on the counter. On the kitchen table, I had put out our ingredients, measuring cups, measuring spoons, cupcake tins, and everything else we needed.

"Mmm, I smell chili," Emma said as she came into the kitchen.

"Spicy?" Alexis asked.

"Hot sauce is on the side," I promised her. "We can eat now if you want."

"Let's get the batter started," Alexis suggested.

"We've got a lot of cupcakes to bake. And then we have to try to get a perfect *R* logo on each cupcake without Mia here."

"It's just one letter," Emma said. "I think we can handle it."

Alexis leaned in and whispered to me. "Where's your mom?"

"Upstairs, I think," I whispered back. "Why?"

"I need the supplies for the proposal cupcakes," she said. "Emma and I are going to bake them tomorrow morning, so we won't have much to do after the magazine launch tomorrow night."

I nodded. "Right." Alexis had mentioned that at lunch yesterday. I had the bag stashed away in the pantry off the kitchen, and I brought it out.

"Perfect," she said, and her eyes were twinkling.

"So, you know what Jeff is planning?" I asked.

"We do, and it's soooo incredibly sweet!" Emma chimed in.

"No fair!" I said. "You guys know and I don't."

"It's better if you're surprised," Alexis said. "Trust me!"

I sighed. I knew Alexis wasn't going to spill the beans, and Emma wouldn't do it if Alexis was around. I would just have to wait until tomorrow to find out what would happen.

"I'll grate the zucchini," I said, launching into cupcake mode.

"I'll mix the wet ingredients," said Emma.

"And I'll get the dry ones going," added Alexis.

We got to work then, and quickly put together batter for two dozen zucchini cupcakes.

"One of these days we'll be able to afford a commercial mixer," Alexis said as we prepared to start all over for the next two dozen.

"And a commercial kitchen, with a cupcake shop attached," I added.

"With pale pink walls, and little tables for people to sit at and eat their cupcakes, with stools that look like cupcakes," said Emma.

"That would be amazing!" I said. "I can just picture it."

"We'd have to think of a name for the shop," said Alexis. "I don't think we could call it the Cupcake Club."

I shook my head. "No, don't you see? It's perfect! A club is a cool place where people go to hang out. So the Cupcake Club is where people could go and eat cupcakes."

Alexis nodded thoughtfully. "And we could have an actual club that you could join if you're a repeat customer, and everybody could get, like, a membership card or a T-shirt. That would be great marketing. Everyone would want to be a member!"

"Wouldn't that be so cool if it were real?" Emma asked dreamily.

The timer went off, and I checked on the first batch of cupcakes by inserting a toothpick into one of them. It came out clean.

"First batch done," I said, using oven mitts to remove the two cupcake tins and put them on cooling racks.

"Two more going in!" Alexis called out.

We kept working until we had a batch of avocado icing in the fridge, four dozen cupcakes cooling, and two dozen more in the oven with a timer on. By then, my stomach was growling.

"Chili break!" I yelled, and we all fixed our chili how we liked it (lots of everything for me; no hot sauce or cheese for Alexis; cheese, chips, and a little bit of hot sauce for Emma). Then we brought our bowls to the kitchen table.

At that moment the doorbell rang.

"I'll get it!" I heard Mom call out.

She came into the kitchen a minute later, followed by Jeff and Emily.

"Hey there, Cupcake Club," Jeff said.

"Jeff and Emily were at the middle school

football game, and I told them to stop by for some chili," Mom explained.

"It smells great," said Jeff. "And so do your cupcakes."

"Katie, get the extra chairs from the pantry, please," Mom instructed.

I took the two folding chairs that we use when we have more than four people around our table while Mom helped Jeff and Emily fix their bowls of chili. Soon, we were all sitting around and eating and talking.

Then the timer went off, and Mom helped me take the last two cupcake tins out of the oven. Jeff stood up.

"Sorry, we didn't mean to interrupt an important baking session," he said.

"Well, it's not our most important baking session this weekend," Emma said, and you could tell she was bursting with the secret of the proposal. Jeff winked at her.

I glanced at Mom. She was talking to Emily and hadn't heard or noticed. Whew!

We all cleaned up the chili dishes together. Then we said good-bye to Jeff and Emily and got back to work on the cupcakes. We iced them with the avocado buttercream and then started drawing the *R* logo on them with frosting pens.

Mom came in to see what we were doing, and frowned. "Are you sure that avocado will hold up until tomorrow?"

"There's tons of lemon juice in the icing, so it should," I said, but I felt nervous.

"Oh great! We're going to serve rotten avocado cupcakes," Emma moaned.

"They'll be fine," Alexis said. "We'll keep them in the refrigerator until tomorrow night. We can use the big one in my basement."

I looked at the cupcakes. They did look kind of cool, with the bright green and red, but now Mom had me worried. But there was nothing we could do. We packed up the cupcakes into their special carriers, and then Alexis called her mom. It was chilly out, and I shivered as we brought the carriers outside and loaded them carefully into the trunk of Mrs. Becker's van.

"This is going to be an exciting weekend," Emma teased as she climbed into the van. Alexis's mom was going to drop off Emma on the way home.

I shivered again, but not from the cold. Jeff's proposal was definitely going to happen this weekend. Life was changing so fast that I couldn't keep up!

# CHAPTER 12

## Hurting

𝓘 fell into bed exhausted that night, and the next morning I woke up groggy when the alarm announced that it was six thirty. I hit the snooze button, but only once. I wasn't about to be late for my second day of work.

Mom was already awake and drinking coffee when I got to the kitchen. I could tell by the way she was dressed that she was working that day.

"I'll drop you off, and Jeff and Emily will pick you up at noon, if that's okay," Mom said. "I've got patients until one o'clock."

"Sure," I said.

She got me to the restaurant just before eight again, and this time she didn't come in with me, just waited until she saw that I got inside. I didn't even see Marc Donald Brown, but Melissa smiled when I walked into the kitchen.

"Katie! Thank goodness," she said. "Put on your apron. We've got a bushel of apples to dice."

"More tarts?" I asked, tying my apron strings behind me.

"No, apple cake this time," she said. "With vanilla ice cream and caramel sauce."

"That sounds amazing," I said.

"But first, apples," she said. "Peeled, cored, and diced. Let me see how you handle a knife."

I picked up a knife she had laid out for me and held it in my right hand, being careful to keep my pointer and middle fingers tucked under my thumb.

"Looks good," she said. "Let me guess. Did you learn that at cooking camp too?"

I grinned. "Yeah."

"Wow, I wish they'd had that when I was kid," she said. "Okay, then, I need the apples diced."

She picked up an apple, and in seconds flat she peeled it, cored it with her knife, and diced it into pieces that looked like little building blocks of exactly the same size.

I could feel my eyes get wide. "There is no way I can do it that fast," I said.

"You don't have to," she said. "Every apple you chop is one I don't have to do."

I started peeling, coring, and chopping. Melissa worked next to me. I took my time with the first one, trying to make sure I got the apple pieces all the same size. By the time I was done, I saw that Melissa had finished three!

So I tried to work faster, and that was my mistake. The freshly washed apple under my fingertips was slippery, and my left hand holding it slipped just as I was cutting through the apple with my right hand.

I felt a sharp pain in my left pointer finger, and when I looked down, I saw blood oozing out. I quickly stepped back from the worktable.

"Um, Melissa," I said, gripping my injured finger. "I need some help over here."

Melissa took one look at me and realized what had happened.

"Oh boy, we've got a bleeder!" she said. "Come on, let's get to the sink. We have a first-aid kit."

I followed her to the sink. My finger was hurting really bad. She ran some cold water over it, and then she frowned.

"That looks pretty deep," she said. "I think you're going to need stitches, Katie."

"Stitches?" I felt the blood drain from my face. I'd never had stitches before. It was a scary thought.

Melissa turned to a guy walking past with a plastic tub. "Get Don for me," she said. Then she took a clean towel and wrapped it around my finger. "Keep pressure on it with your right hand," she instructed me.

"I'm so sorry!" I blurted out. "There are all these apples to cut, and I—"

"You mean you never cut yourself at cooking camp?" Melissa asked, and I shook my head. "Well, it's about time! Everybody who works in a kitchen gets sliced, diced, burned, and banged up. It's part of the job. You'll get sewed up and you'll be fine. And if you're lucky, you'll have a cool little scar to remind you of it."

She held up her left hand and showed me a scar on her palm. "That was a fun one," she said. "Luckily, I missed my tendons."

Marc Donald Brown walked in. "Melissa, what's— Oh, hi, Katie! Is everything okay?"

"She needs stitches," Melissa said. "You need to get her to the emergency room or an urgent care center."

Marc Donald Brown ran his hand through his hair. "Oh man, we're getting ready for the lunch rush right now. Katie, can you call your mother?"

"Uh, yeah, I guess," I said.

"Okay, good," he said. "Let me know if you need anything, okay?"

He hurried off, and I saw Melissa shaking her head.

"Okay, let's get your mom on the phone," she said. I took my cell out of my pocket, and she took it from me. "What's the number under? 'Home'?"

"'Mom Work,'" I said, returning my right hand to put pressure on my left. Blood was starting to seep through the towel.

"Uh, hi, this is Melissa Stackman, and I'm here at Chez Donald with Katie," Melissa said. "Can I please speak to her mom?"

Melissa listened and then put the phone on speaker so I could hear too.

"Katie!" It was Joanne. "Your mom's in the middle of a difficult extraction right now. Is everything okay?"

"I cut my finger, and Melissa says I need stitches, and it's bleeding a lot, and I need her to take me," I said as hot tears sprung up in my eyes.

"Oh, poor sweetie! Hold on a sec."

We heard the sounds of classic rock for a few seconds, and then Joanne's voice came back.

"Hon, Jeff's going to come get you," she said. "Hold tight."

"Okay," I said, and Melissa ended the call.

"Come on, sweetie. Let's wait outside."

It seemed like forever before Jeff pulled up, but it was probably only a few minutes. There were no parking spaces, but he put his hazard lights on and rolled down the window. Then he got out and opened the passenger door for me.

"Don't worry, Katie!" Melissa called out to me. "It only hurts a little bit. You'll be back in the kitchen in no time."

Jeff helped me put on my seat belt and then started to drive.

"We're going to St. Claire's Hospital," he said. "Joanne's sister works in the emergency room there. Joanne is faxing over your insurance information and a consent form from your mom."

"A consent form?" I asked.

"Well, you're a minor," Jeff explained. "So a relative needs to bring you in order for the doctors to help you."

*Like a mom. Or a dad,* I thought, and my mind wandered to Marc Donald Brown. I understood why Mom couldn't take me; she was in the middle of wrenching someone's tooth from their jaw. But

MDB? Was the start of the lunch rush so important that he couldn't bring me himself? I guess it was more important than me.

Jeff glanced over at my toweled hand. "Does it hurt?" he asked.

"It's throbbing, mostly," I said. "I just feel so stupid. My second day on the job, and I made a dumb mistake."

"I'm sure it happens to the best of chefs," Jeff said.

"Yeah, that's what Melissa said." Then I realized something—Emily wasn't in the car. "Where's Emily?" I asked.

"She's got a soccer game this morning, and then she's spending the afternoon with her friend Abby," Jeff explained. "But she'll be coming with me and your mom later to the magazine launch party."

"You're coming?" I asked, a little bit surprised.

"Sure. I'm looking forward to seeing my cupcake bakers in action," he said.

That was really nice of him, I thought, although part of me was a little worried. I hadn't told Mom that I'd invited Marc Donald Brown. And now my real dad was going to be in the same room as my soon-to-be stepdad. It sounded like a perfect recipe for awkwardness.

I knew I would have to tell Mom, but I didn't have much time to dwell on it because we had reached the hospital. Jeff pulled into the emergency room parking lot, and my heart started to beat a little faster as I remembered what I was here for.

Jeff walked me inside.

"St. Claire's is a small hospital, and a little less hectic than County General," he told me. "Things should go pretty smoothly."

We walked up to the desk to sign in, and Jeff gave my name. The woman behind the desk had curly red hair that reminded me of Alexis.

"Oh, Katie! Joanne called and told me you were coming," she said. "I'm her sister, Brittany. Don't worry, hon. Take a seat, and we'll bring you in as soon as we can."

Brittany had such a friendly smile that I felt a little less nervous. She handed Jeff a clipboard, and then we went to the waiting room. There were about five people waiting there, and Jeff and I found seats next to each other. Jeff started filling out paperwork, and I tried to distract myself by watching someone install flooring in a home improvement show on the TV. Not exactly thrilling, but it took my mind off my throbbing finger.

I nervously tapped my sneaker on the floor until

they called me in. Brittany took me into a room with only curtains for walls and had me sit on this metal table.

"The doctor should be right in," she said. "Don't worry. Dr. DeNonno is great with a needle."

I looked at Jeff. "Did she say needle?" I asked as Brittany walked away.

"You'll probably need a few stitches, Katie," Jeff said. "It's not so bad, honestly. When I was your age, I fell off my bike and had to get seventeen stitches on my forehead. You'll probably only need a few."

I nodded, too nervous to talk. Then a woman with short, dark hair came in. Her name tag read DR. DENONNO.

"Hi, Katie," she said. "So, I hear you've cut your finger pretty badly?"

"I guess so," I said. "I didn't really get a good look at it. But it was bleeding a lot."

"Let's take a look," she said. She gently took my left hand and removed the towel. After a few seconds, she nodded.

"You're going to need a few stitches," she said. "It's a good thing your dad brought you here."

"Oh, he's not my dad," I said. "He's my . . ." I didn't know how to explain. He wasn't my stepdad yet. He wasn't even officially my future stepdad—at

111

least not until my mom said yes to his proposal.

"I'm her mom's boyfriend," Jeff explained.

"Well, either way, it's a good thing you're here," Dr. DeNonno said. "So, I'm going to clean up your wound, and then I'm going to use a needle to numb the tip of your finger. That part will hurt for just a second. Then you won't even feel me giving you the stitches. All right?"

"Okay," I said weakly. She had lost me at the word "needle."

"Also, I see from your chart that you're due for a tetanus shot," she said. "We'll take care of that, too."

*Oh great. Another needle!* I thought. But I didn't say anything. I didn't want Dr. DeNonno to think I was a baby.

Jeff grabbed my right hand. "Squeeze my hand if it hurts, Katie, okay?" he said, and I gave a little squeeze.

Brittany came in to assist the doctor. She gave me another big smile. "You'll be out of here soon, sweetie."

And then Dr. DeNonno got to work. I get queasy thinking about the whole thing, but she did give me a tiny shot in my finger and she was right—I didn't feel the stitches after the shot. I wish I could say the same for the tetanus shot. That hurt!

When we left the hospital, I had a bandage on my finger and another little one on my arm, where I'd gotten the shot. It didn't hurt though.

"Is your right hand still working?" Jeff asked.

I looked at him curiously. "Why wouldn't it?" I asked.

"Just wanted to make sure," he said. "Because you'll need it to hold an ice-cream cone."

I couldn't believe how nice Jeff was being! He was doing everything Mom would have done, and more, because I got a pumpkin-fudge ice-cream cone on the way home.

When we pulled up to my house, Mom was waiting outside.

"Katie!" she cried, running up to me. "I'm so sorry I couldn't get away. Are you okay?"

"I'm fine," I replied.

She looked at Jeff. "Thank you so much."

"You know I'd do anything for Katie," he said, and I got a little lump in my throat then.

"So, honey, will you be okay to go to the magazine launch tonight?" Mom asked.

"It's just one finger," I replied. "I should be fine." And then I remembered something—I needed to tell her that I had invited MDB to the magazine launch.

I was about to tell her when my phone rang. It was Marc Donald Brown. I was surprised.

"Katie, how's your finger?" he asked.

"Three stitches," I said.

"Glad you're okay," he said. "So, listen, I'm sorry, but I can't make the magazine thing tonight. Cecile and Ella have a dance recital, and I forgot about it. But maybe we can make plans to do something else soon."

"Sure," I said.

Then MDB hung up.

"Was that your dad? What did he want?" Mom asked.

"He was just checking on me," I replied.

I didn't tell her that I had invited him to the launch or that he had bailed on me. Strangely, I didn't feel upset about it.

*Why?* I wondered. Why wasn't I feeling upset? But I didn't have time to really think about it—I had to start getting ready for the magazine launch!

# CHAPTER 13

## Emma Saves the Day

$\mathcal{M}$om dropped me off at Alexis's house at five o'clock. Inside her kitchen, I found Alexis, Emma, and Mia, staring sadly at a container of cupcakes on the counter.

"What's wrong?" I asked.

"It's the avocado buttercream," said Alexis. "It's kind of . . ."

"Icky," Mia chimed in. "The green isn't exactly brown, but it's not bright green anymore. It's almost . . ."

"Diaper green," Emma finished. "Trust me: I know from changing Jake's diapers."

"That can't be good," I said, and I walked over to examine the cupcakes. They were right. The frosting was a dull green, and it wasn't fluffy like icing.

I frowned. "I thought the lemon juice and the sugar would keep the avocado fresh. But I guess this frosting works best if you eat it the same day."

"They're not *so* bad," Alexis said.

"Maybe it will be dark in the room," I suggested.

"Wait here," Emma said.

She walked out of the kitchen and came back in holding three cupcake carriers.

"What's that?" Alexis asked.

"Three dozen vanilla cupcakes with vanilla icing," Emma said. "I baked them late last night, after I got home. I was worried that not everybody would like the green cupcakes."

Mia hugged her. "Oh, Emma! You saved us!"

Alexis frowned. "It's a good idea, but then what's our story? How are these cupcakes trendy?"

"Simplicity," Mia said. "White is classic in fashion. Vanilla is classic in cooking."

"I can work with that," said Alexis. "We can put out three dozen of each kind, and that way we can appeal to the adventurous eaters as well as the safe ones."

"That should work," I said. "Sorry, I didn't think that doing the avocado in advance could be a problem. I guess I've had a lot on my mind lately."

That's when Mia noticed my bandaged finger.

"Oh wow! Katie, what happened to your finger?"

"Oh, I cut myself at the restaurant," I explained, and then I told my friends the story. I got major hugs for that! Then it was time to pack up the cupcakes and head to the venue. Alexis's dad took us in his van.

The party was being held at Ice, a former ice-skating-rink-turned-party-space in Stonebrook. We unloaded the van and walked in carrying our cupcakes, business cards, and flyers. (I should mention that we were all wearing our official Cupcake Club uniforms—black pants and our official T-shirts.)

Alex walked up to a table labeled CATERING CHECK-IN. The woman behind it gave Alex a curious look.

"Alex Becker of the Cupcake Club," Alexis said in her most businesslike voice.

The woman raised an eyebrow and checked her list. Then she nodded. "You're in that corner over there," she said, pointing to a table.

"Thank you," Alexis said.

As we made our way to the table, I looked around, wide-eyed. There was a big banner across the back wall that read RELISH NJ. Round tables with black tablecloths lined the walls, and each one had the name of a different caterer or restaurant written on a small chalkboard standing on the table.

"This is the most professional event we've ever been invited to," I said in awe. "Look, there's Lotus Sushi over there! They make the best sushi!"

"And we make the best cupcakes," Alexis said confidently.

Alexis had packed up our black cupcake tiers, which matched the slick décor perfectly. We quickly worked to arrange our cupcakes artfully on the tiers. Then Mia used her best handwriting to write our cupcake titles on the chalkboard:

"Green with Envy"

"Classic Vanilla"

"'Green with Envy,'" I said. "That's pretty cool."

"Emma and I thought that up this morning, when we were baking the proposal cupcakes," Alexis said.

"I almost forgot—that's tomorrow!" I cried. "Come on! You've got to tell me what Jeff is planning."

"I absolutely do not," Alexis said with a wicked grin. "Okay, we've got to look alive! People are coming in."

A small jazz band began to play, and people started to enter the space. It was a pretty cool setup. You could walk around and get small bites of food from each of the tables. Everything looked so good!

My stomach rumbled. "I hope there'll be some sushi left over."

I spotted Mom coming in with Jeff and Emily, who was wearing a cute pink dress. Mom and Jeff were pretty dressed up too. Jeff had on a blue suit and a green tie, and Mom had on her favorite black dress.

I waved them over to our table.

"You guys look so nice!" I said.

Emily held out the necklace she was wearing to show me. "I wore my cupcake necklace, Katie," she said.

"How are you feeling?" Mom asked.

"Well, I could use some sushi," I said. "Could you please bring me some?"

"On it!" said Jeff, and he hustled away. Mom and Emily followed him.

Then I heard a loud voice.

"*Mija!*"

It was Mia's dad. (He calls her "*mija*," which is short for "my daughter" in Spanish, and it sounds just like her name.) Behind him were her mom and her stepfather, Eddie.

Mia's dad gave her a hug. "What a nice event this is. You guys have made it to the big time."

"There's so much food!" Eddie said. "I'm going to start at one end and get something from every table."

"Don't forget to get a cupcake," Mia said. "You can do us a favor and take one of our green cupcakes. They're a little . . . sad."

Eddie picked up one along with a small plate. "They don't look sad to me!"

"Ix-nay on the ad-say," said Alexis. "We want people to think all our cupcakes are fabulous!"

Mia's parents (all three of them) went off to get food, and we got to work handing out cupcakes. Alexis was talking a mile a minute.

"Our Green with Envy cupcake is delicious and healthy," she would say to anyone who passed by. "And our Classic Vanilla is simply timeless."

Some people made a face when they saw the green cupcake, and picked the vanilla. But just as many were excited about the green cupcake.

"I love this idea," one woman said, taking a bite. "It's got fiber, healthy fats—and even chocolate!"

"Tell your friends about us," Alexis said, giving her a business card.

We were busy giving out cupcakes for about an hour. When things slowed down, Mia took me aside.

"This has been a crazy day for you, hasn't it?" she asked. "I feel so bad that you got stitches."

I nodded. "Yeah, it didn't hurt as much as I thought," I said. "It was just weird because my dad didn't take me to the hospital. And then he was supposed to come tonight, but he bailed."

"Oh, Katie! That stinks," Mia said.

"Kind of," I said, but then I spotted Jeff across the room. He and Mom were talking and laughing. "It was okay, though. Jeff took me."

"Yeah, stepfathers can be pretty nice," said Mia. "I'm lucky, I guess. I don't get to see my dad every day, but I know Eddie is always there for me."

I thought about how Jeff had held my hand in the emergency room that day. "I guess I'm pretty lucky too," I said, and then I remembered something. "Now all Mom has to do is say yes tomorrow!"

# CHAPTER 14

## Will You Marry Me?

The next morning I woke up with a tingling feeling, and it wasn't in my finger. I was so excited to find out how Jeff was going to propose to Mom and what she would say!

I got a clue when I went down to the kitchen. Mom was dressed and drinking coffee.

"You're up early," she remarked.

"Yeah, it's a nice day out," I said.

"Jeff asked if we wanted to go on a run with him and Emily later this morning," Mom said. "I told him okay. Is that okay with you? You can stay here if you want."

"No, I'll go!" I said, and looked at the clock. It was only eight o'clock. "I'll make some scrambled eggs. Protein for the run."

"Sounds good," Mom said.

So I cooked breakfast, and then I folded laundry, and then I read a chapter of the book we're reading for English. The morning seemed to go on forever. Finally, Mom said it was time to meet Jeff and Emily at the park.

We ran there, like we always do, and we found Jeff and Emily by the park entrance. Emily had a big smile on her face.

"Morning, sunshines," Jeff said. "Let's keep moving. It's a beautiful day!"

He was right. The morning air was chilly, but it was the good kind of chilly, the kind that makes you feel alive and keeps you awake. The sky was blue, and the green grass was littered with orange leaves.

Jeff stayed in the lead as we jogged down the path. After a few minutes we came to the park gazebo, where people can have picnics overlooking the pond.

"Hey, let's check out the gazebo," Jeff said suddenly, and he veered off the path and ran on the grass toward it.

"Jeff, where are you going?" Mom called out, and Emily and I looked at each other and grinned. We both had an idea what was happening.

Jeff stopped in front of a picnic table under the gazebo that was decorated with a pretty white tablecloth with green flowers. The table was set with four plates and four napkins that matched the tablecloth, and it was topped with a grilled vegetable platter, a tray of mini sandwiches, and a bowl of colorful fruit salad. There was also a clear pitcher of pink lemonade and four plastic cups shaped like wineglasses.

"Looks like it's lunchtime," Jeff said. "Come on—sit down."

"Jeff, what's going on?" Mom asked as she took her seat. "Who did this?"

I had an idea. I looked around the park for Mia, Emma, and Alexis, but I couldn't see them.

"Let's eat," Jeff said.

I put a tiny egg salad sandwich on my plate, along with some vegetables and fruit.

"This is all from Schreiber's Deli," Mom said. "I love their food."

"I know," said Jeff, with a twinkle in his eyes.

Nobody talked much as we ate. Emily and I knew what was going to happen, and Mom was suspicious, taking it all in. When we finished lunch, Jeff started talking in a loud voice.

"That was a great lunch," he said. His voice got

even louder. "This would be a great time for some dessert!"

A few seconds later, Mia, Alexis, and Emma came walking up, holding a big white box. They placed it in front of Mom.

"Open it," Jeff said.

Mom gave Jeff an almost frightened look. She slowly opened up the box lid. Emily and I both jumped up and ran next to her so we could see.

Inside the box were rows of cupcakes spelling out "Will You Marry Me?" The extra cupcakes were decorated with tiny pink and brown flowers, green leaves, and winding stems. My friends had done an amazing job!

"'Will you marry me?'" Mom whispered.

Jeff got down on one knee. He took a box from his pocket. Then he opened it. A ring with a heart-shaped diamond glittered inside.

"Will you, Sharon?" he asked.

I held my breath. I was pretty sure Mom was going to say yes, but I wasn't sure. Her first marriage had been pretty bad after all, and—

"Yes!" Mom cried, and she fell into Jeff's arms.

Suddenly, me and my friends and Emily were all jumping up and down and squealing and hugging one another.

After we calmed down, Mom turned to me. "Did you know about this?" she asked, wiping a tear from her eye.

"Most of it," I said.

Then Mom's eyes got wide. "Oh, Katie, I shouldn't have said yes without talking to you first. I mean, this will affect your life too, and—"

I stopped her. "Mom, it's okay! I say yes too."

"And me too!" said Emily, and she was so sweet when she said that that I had to hug her.

Jeff stood up and looked at Emily and me. "I have something for you both, as well," he said.

Emily and I exchanged curious glances. Jeff held out a small box to each of us. We took them and opened them at the same time.

Inside my box was a necklace with a silver chain and a pendant with the outline of a heart, embedded with little sparkly purple gems. I looked at Emily's. Her necklace was the same, except the gems on her heart were sky blue.

"I just want you both to know that you are special to me," Jeff said. "When I marry Sharon, we'll become a family. And I'm really excited about that."

Mom started to cry. I felt my eyes tear up too. I hugged Jeff.

"Thanks," I said. "It's beautiful."

"Purple is still your favorite color, right?" Jeff asked, and I nodded. "And, Emily, I know you love sky blue."

Emily put on her necklace. "Katie, put yours on!" she said. "We'll match."

"That's so cute!" Emma said. "You two are like sisters."

"Wow, it's, like, raining sisters lately," I joked. I still wasn't sure how to feel about not being an only child anymore—but so far, it felt pretty nice.

"We have so many ideas for the wedding," Alexis said. "So let us know as soon as you have a date."

Mom sat back down at the table. "A wedding date! My head is spinning. I need a cupcake. We all need a cupcake!"

"Pictures first!" said Mia, and she took photos of Mom and Jeff behind the cupcakes, and one of Mom and Jeff with Emily and me around the cupcakes too.

Then we all sat down and started eating cupcakes.

"Wow, this mocha is delicious," I said.

Just then I got a text. It was Marc Donald Brown: Hey, Katie. How u doing?

Good, I texted back. I was actually much better than good, but I couldn't tell him why.

Melissa and I are hoping you can come again Saturday. We can make it a regular thing, he wrote.

I didn't text back right away. I knew I liked working in the restaurant. And I definitely liked Melissa. But working at the restaurant would mean that Marc Donald Brown would definitely be part of my life. I had to think about that.

*You can see him as much or as little as you want,* Mom had told me. I looked at the cupcakes, and then it hit me—my dad was like a cupcake.

I know that sounds weird, but see—Marc Donald Brown would never be a breakfast-lunch-and-dinner dad. He wasn't even a meat-and-potato dad. He was a dessert dad. You don't have dessert every day, but when you do, it's nice.

Sounds good, I texted him back. I knew I could work at the restaurant without feeling weird. Because for me and Marc Donald Brown—my dad—for now, it would be just desserts.

Want another sweet cupcake?

Here's a sneak peek

of the next book in the

# CUPCAKE  DIARIES

series:

# Mia

# measures

# up

## Life Happens!

*I* shouldn't have eaten that third corn dog," my friend Katie Brown moaned. We were strapped inside a round blue chair on an amusement park ride, and we just kept spinning . . . spinning . . . and spinning. . . .

I looked over at her. Her brown ponytail was whipping back and forth, and her skin looked positively green. (Although that may have been caused by the flashing lights on the ride.)

"Don't puke on me! I just got these sneakers!" I warned her, laughing, and I saw Katie's knuckles tightly grip the bar in front of us.

"Don't say that word!" Katie yelled.

Luckily for both of us, the ride slowed to a stop. Katie and I climbed off. My legs felt wobbly.

"That was a close one," Katie said, leaning against a tree. "Whew!"

I looked at my phone. "It's almost five. We should get back to the table."

Katie nodded. "Right."

It was a beautiful twilight, and Katie and I were with our friends Alexis Becker and Emma Taylor at the Maple Grove Carnival. The four of us own a business together, the Cupcake Club. A few weeks ago Alexis had submitted a vendor application to the carnival so that we could sell our cupcakes there, and they'd accepted us!

"I like that we're taking shifts," Katie said as we walked past a bouncy house with little kids going crazy inside. "I'm glad I had a chance to go on the rides."

"Even the Whirling Twirler?" I asked.

"Yes," Katie insisted. "In fact, I could go for another corn dog about now." She started looking around.

"Absolutely not!" I said. I grabbed her by the arm and started running toward our cupcake booth.

"But I love corn dogs!" Katie yelled behind me. "I would marry one if I could!"

We were both laughing so hard that I bumped right into someone. Luckily, it was someone we knew—it was our friend George Martinez.

"Hey! The bumper cars are over there," George said, pointing.

"Sorry," I said.

Katie bumped into him too. "My turn!"

"Ouch! You're jabbing me with your pointy elbows!" George teased.

Katie and George are friends—the kind of friends who would be boyfriend and girlfriend if they were old enough to go on dates. So they're not boyfriend and girlfriend, but they do hang out together sometimes.

"Anyway, I'm doing serious business here," George said, nodding to the booth in front of us. "I need to buy my ticket to win the tickets to the La Vida Pasa concert before they do the drawing."

I nodded. "I bought mine earlier! So you might as well not bother buying your ticket, because I'm going to win."

"Wait, La Vida Pasa?" Katie asked. "What does that mean? 'Life passes'?"

"More like the saying, 'life happens,'" I replied. "Come on, you've heard me play them before. They're so good!"

"Oh, yeah," Katie said. "They sing all in Spanish, right?"

"*Sí, amiga,*" George answered. "And they are *muy bueno.*"

He pulled some cash out of his pocket. "And now, if you'll excuse me, I need to buy the *winning* ticket."

"And we'd better get back to the table," Katie said.

"Good luck!" I called to George as we left. "You're going to need it."

Normally, I'm not a person who teases, but George teases everybody all the time (well, mostly Katie), so I thought I should dish it back to him for once.

Our little booth wasn't far away. My stepdad, Eddie, had set up a tent for us, and the park had provided everyone with tables. Our table had a pink tablecloth with our cupcake logo on the front.

Emma was handing a cupcake to a customer, and Alexis was putting change into our cashbox.

"How are we doing?" Katie asked after the customer walked away.

"We sold sixteen more while you were gone!" Emma announced. "I think we'll sell out before this ends at six."

"We'll sell the last hour, if you two want to go do the rides," I said.

Emma looked at Alexis, and they both nodded.

"Whatever you do, don't eat three corn dogs before you go on the Whirling Twirler," Katie warned them.

Alexis's green eyes got wide. "Did you really do that?"

"Not my smartest decision," Katie replied.

"Well, I was thinking of getting a funnel cake," Emma said. "But maybe I'll do that after the rides."

"Mmmm, funnel cake," Katie said, and then she put her arms out in front of her and started to zombie-walk toward the funnel cake stand.

Once again, I grabbed her. "You're not going anywhere," I said. I took a look at the table. "We've got two dozen cupcakes left to sell."

"We sold out of the vanilla with rainbow sprinkles," Alexis reported. "But we always do. We need to push the maple walnut ones."

"Those are the best ones!" Katie said. "Maple walnut cupcakes for the Maple Grove carnival. People need to be more adventurous with their cupcake choices."

"Hey, it's the Cupcake Sisters!"

We turned to see my cousin Sebastian and my stepbrother, Dan. Sebastian was the one who had called us the Cupcake Sisters.

"We're the Cupcake Club, not Cupcake Sisters," I told him.

"But you look like sisters," he said.

I shook my head. Katie, Alexis, Emma, and I didn't look anything alike. I've got stick-straight black hair and dark brown eyes. Katie's got wavy, light brown hair that matches her eyes. Emma is blond haired and blue eyed, and Alexis is a green-eyed redhead.

"Just because we're all wearing the same T-shirt and we all have our hair in ponytails doesn't mean we look like sisters," I said.

Sebastian shrugged. "It's just my opinion."

"Yeah, he's, um, entitled to his opinion," Emma said awkwardly, and then she blushed a little bit.

"Come on, Emma. Let's get to the rides before they close," Alexis said, stepping out from behind the table. "We'll be back at six to help clean up!"

Katie and I got behind the table, and Dan reached for a chocolate cupcake.

"That'll be three dollars," I said.

"Really?" Dan asked. "I used to be your official cupcake taster, remember? Doesn't that count for something?"

"These cupcakes have already passed the taste test," I said. "Besides, you've got all that sweet pizza delivery money. You can afford a cupcake."

Dan rolled his eyes and fished in his pocket for the cash. Katie took it from him.

"What about me?" asked Sebastian. "I'm too young to deliver pizza."

Sebastian is a freshman in high school, and Dan is a senior. Sebastian moved here a little while ago from Puerto Rico, and he and Dan bonded over death metal music, so they hang out all the time now.

Dan handed Katie another three dollars. "One more cupcake, please."

"Get the maple walnut," Katie said. "It's the best one."

Sebastian smiled. "Sure." He picked one up and bit into it. "Yeah, that's good."

Then Dan and Sebastian walked off, and Katie started hawking our cupcakes.

"Homemade cupcakes here! Get your maple walnut cupcakes!" she yelled.

A couple came over right away, and each of them bought a maple walnut cupcake.

"Keep going, Katie. It's working," I told her.

Katie moved to the front of the table.

"Get your cupcakes here!" she sang, and then she busted out some crazy dance moves.

"Katie, what are you doing?" I asked.

"This is my happy cupcake dance!" she replied.

At that moment a group of girls walked past our booth. To be more specific they were the girls in the BFC (the Best Friends Club): Callie Wilson, Maggie Rodriguez, Olivia Allen, and Bella Kovacs.

"Nice dance, Katie," Olivia said in the most sarcastic voice possible, and the other girls giggled.

"Thank you!" Katie replied, still dancing. Most of us had learned to just ignore the behavior of the Best Friends Club.

Callie broke away from the others. "I'll have a chocolate cupcake, please," she said.

Now, maybe Callie just wanted a cupcake. Or maybe she did it because she and Katie used to be best friends before middle school, and I know that Callie feels bad when the other BFC girls are mean to Katie. Either way, it was nice of her.

I handed Callie her chocolate cupcake and then checked my phone.

"It's almost five thirty," I told Katie. "They're going to announce the winner of the concert tickets. I'm just going to get closer to the stage so I can hear, okay?"

Katie nodded. "Sure, I'll be fine."

I quickly made my way to the stage area, where

all the announcements had been made throughout the day. It was almost dark now, and the park lights were shining. I got to the stage just as some members of the high school music club were getting to the microphone. I quickly took my ticket out of my pocket.

"We'd like to thank everyone who purchased a raffle ticket today. All proceeds are going to the music club," a girl was saying.

Then a boy picked a ticket out of a bag. "And the winner is . . . ticket 306978."

I stared at the ticket in my hand: 306978. The numbers were right there in front of me. I couldn't believe it. I'd won!

I ran up to the stage. "I think I have the winning ticket," I said, handing it to the girl. I still couldn't believe it was true.

She and the boy checked the numbers. Then the boy handed me a white envelope.

"Congratulations! You've won two tickets to see La Vida Pasa!"

I held back a scream of joy. "Thank you!"

As I raced back to tell Katie the good news, I passed George. He gave me the evil eye, but I knew he was only kidding.

"Sorry, George. Life happens," I told him, and

then I excitedly ran to the Cupcake Club booth.

"Katie! I won! I won the tickets!" I yelled, waving the envelope.

Katie started jumping up and down. "Woo-hoo! Good for you!"

"You're coming with me, right?" I asked.

"Well, sure, yeah," she said. "But I don't really know their music."

"It's great!" I said. "We'll have fun."

"And I won't really understand the words," Katie went on.

"That's okay," I said. "You know my Spanish is terrible. I used to think one of their songs was about a lost dog, but it's really about a lost love."

Katie laughed. "All right, I'll go. Thanks—it's nice of you to give me the ticket. When is it?"

"Three weeks from now, on a Friday," I replied. "This is going to be awesome."

"*Sí!*" Katie agreed.

Coco Simon always dreamed of opening a cupcake bakery but was afraid she would eat all of the profits. When she's not daydreaming about cupcakes, Coco edits children's books and has written close to one hundred books for children, tweens, and young adults, which is a lot less than the number of cupcakes she's eaten. Cupcake Diaries is the first time Coco has mixed her love of cupcakes with writing.

# Want more

# CUPCAKE DIARIES?

Visit **CupcakeDiariesBooks.com**
for the series trailer, excerpts, activities,
and everything you need for throwing
your own cupcake party!

# Still Hungry?
## There's always room for another Cupcake!

Katie and the cupcake cure

Mia in the mix

Emma on thin icing

Alexis and the perfect recipe

Katie, batter up!

Mia's baker's dozen

CUPCAKE DIARIES — Emma, lights! camera! cupcakes!

CUPCAKE DIARIES — Alexis the icing on the cupcake
by Coco Simon

CUPCAKE DIARIES — Katie starting from scratch

CUPCAKE DIARIES — Mia's recipe for disaster

CUPCAKE DIARIES — Emma's not-so-sweet dilemma

CUPCAKE DIARIES — Alexis's cupcake cupid

CUPCAKE DIARIES — Katie sprinkled secrets
by Coco Simon

CUPCAKE DIARIES — Mia the way the cupcake crumbles

CUPCAKE DIARIES — Emma raining cats and dogs... and cupcakes!
by Coco Simon

CUPCAKE DIARIES — Alexis cupcake crush
by Coco Simon

CUPCAKE DIARIES — Katie just desserts

CUPCAKE DIARIES — Mia measures up

If you liked

# CUPCAKE  DIARIES

be sure to check out these

other series from

Simon Spotlight

# THE HIDDEN WORLD OF
# Changers

In this electrifying new fantasy series, four normal seventh graders find out that they are Changers, a line of mythological shapeshifters that history has forgotten.

But there's little time for questions. A powerful warlock is racing toward their town, destroying everything in his wake. Can Mack, Gabriella, Darren, and Fiona harness their newfound powers in time to save their home?

## Find out in The Hidden World of Changers series!

If you like reading about
the adventures of Katie, Mia,
Emma, and Alexis, you'll love
Alex and Ava, stars of the
It Takes Two series!

# sew zoey

Zoey's clothing design blog puts her on the A-list in the fashion world . . . but when it comes to school, will she be teased, or will she be a trendsetter? Find out in the Sew Zoey series:

EBOOK EDITIONS ALSO AVAILABLE

SewZoeyBooks.com • Published by Simon Spotlight • Kids.SimonandSchuster.com

Looking for another great book?
Find it
**IN THE MIDDLE.**

Fun, fantastic books for kids
in the in-be**TWEEN** age.

IntheMiddleBooks.com

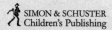